**Jessica tried**

The intervening
mute the bitterne...
any hopes she might secretly have nurtured, that they could at least in the end come to share a tentative friendship, withered and died on the spot. Inside her, the wound of parting that had subsided over the past months to a dull ache throbbed into sharp, pulsing life.

It had been foolish to expect anything more. . .

When **Joanna Neil** discovered Mills & Boon her life-long addiction to reading crystallised into an exciting new career writing medical romances. Her characters are probably the outcome of her varied career, which includes working as a clerk, typist, nurse, and infant teacher. She enjoys dressmaking and cooking at her Leicestershire home. Her family includes a husband, son and daughter, an exuberant yellow Labrador and two slightly crazed cockatiels.

**Recent titles by the same author:**

LOVING REMEDY

# UNEXPECTED COMPLICATIONS

BY

JOANNA NEIL

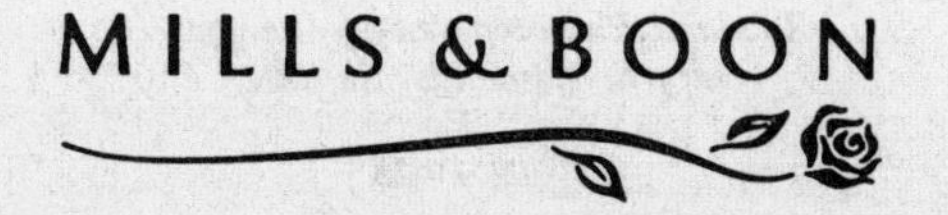

*Harlequin Mills & Boon Limited,*
*Eton House, 18-24 Paradise Road, Richmond, Surrey TW9 1SR*



ISBN 0 263 79467 9

*Set in Times 11 on 12 pt. by*
*Rowland Phototypesetting Limited*
*Bury St Edmunds, Suffolk*

*03-9602-43628*

*Made and printed in Great Britain*
*Cover illustration by Neal Puddephatt*

## CHAPTER ONE

'JESSY-JESSY, where've you been?'

Making sure her bicycle was well secured in the parking slot at the back of the Soar Bridge Health Centre, Jessica Reid turned as her ears caught the gleeful childish tones. A smile lifted the corners of her mouth as she watched the small boy come running joyfully towards her, and she bent down, holding out her arms to him in readiness.

'Hello, Daniel, you little scamp,' she said cheerfully, gathering him up against the soft wool of her winter coat and planting a firm kiss on his cheek. 'My word, I think you've grown, and in just a few weeks, too. Did you miss me? I missed you.' Straightening, she swung him around, then hugged him tightly against the cold February air.

'You've been gone for *ages*,' he complained, his pink mouth jutting, and then, with all the ingenuousness of youth, added, 'Did you bring me a present? You promised.'

Jessica laughed. 'I did, monster. How could I possibly forget?'

Across the car park, Dr Sarah Prentiss finished locking up her Metro and came to join them, a battered teddy bear held firmly in one hand.

'Hi, Jessica, how did the course go?' Her glance swept over her son. 'Stop searching in Jessica's pockets, Daniel,' she reproved him gently. 'Here, you can hold Benjy yourself,' she added, passing the bear to him. 'Lord, it's cold out here. . .shall we go on inside?' She pushed open the door to the centre and they all trooped into the building, Daniel sliding down to the ground and taking his mother's hand in his.

'It went well,' Jessica said, pulling off her gloves and stuffing them into her pockets. 'Ask me anything about health promotion, and it's there at my fingertips, and I'm all geared up now for any asthma patients who need help or advice.'

'That's great,' Sarah acknowledged. 'We seem to be seeing more and more asthmatics just lately. John Stokes reckons it must be partly down to the increase in traffic on the roads, and all the fumes that go along with it. I'm sure he's right. No one walks very far these days. We ought to follow your example and cycle to work. It certainly puts colour in your cheeks, even on a day like this.'

'Just as long as it doesn't snow,' Jessica commented, looking up at the overcast sky. 'There are only a couple of miles between here and my flat, so it doesn't take much above five minutes and I like to think it keeps me fit.'

'Dr Stokes isn't here any more—'cept sometimes,' Daniel informed her as she shrugged out of her coat and hung it up in the closet.

Freed from the upturned collar of the coat, her glossy chestnut hair swung free, falling in a neat, silken bob to an inch or so below her ears.

'We've got a new doctor now,' Daniel went on. 'He's got a sweetie jar like Dr Stokes's. . .*and* a biscuit tin. . .and when I'm waiting for Mummy he says, Go on, then, dip in, help yourself.'

'This child is forever scoffing,' Sarah said with a rueful smile. 'He's almost four, but you'd think he was twice that, from the amount he puts away. It's a wonder to me that he never puts on any fat. He must burn it off with all his rushing around. He's hardly ever still.'

Thoughtfully, Daniel said, 'Dr Tyler says I'm,' he frowned for a moment, then managed triumphantly, 'trainin' for the 'lympics.' He clenched his arm proudly to show a sprouting muscle. 'You need lots of food for that, Dr Tyler says.'

Intent on straightening her blue nurse's uniform, Jessica paused now, her fingers stilling on the darker blue of her belt, her heart giving a strange little lurch.

'Tyler?' she queried, her green eyes troubled as she looked across at Sarah. Of course, Tyler was a common enough name. There was no reason on earth to imagine that the new doctor was the Tyler she knew. Nick had gone to work in Nottingham, hadn't he? Why should he want to come back here? All the same, her heart had begun to beat just a fraction faster.

'That's right, he started in the New Year while you were away,' Sarah supplied. 'I took to him straight off—he was at medical school with Martyn, you know.'

'Yes, I remember Martyn saying so.'

Jessica frowned. As the new head of the centre after John Stokes had retired, Martyn Lancaster had been keen to bring in someone he knew would fit in well here. She must have misheard the name of his friend when the matter of John's replacement had come up for discussion before

Christmas, otherwise she'd have asked questions back then.

Daniel began to tug at her skirt, looking up at her with eager bright eyes, wide with anticipation.

Collecting herself, she reached in her bag and drew out a small package. 'Here you are, sweetheart. Another one to add to your collection.'

She said it with a smile, affectionately ruffling his gleaming fair hair, but her mind was occupied elsewhere and she only half paid attention to his whoop of joy as he pulled apart the paper wrapping and uncovered a bendy yellow dinosaur, its open mouth full of white plastic teeth.

'He's just a few years younger than Martyn,' Sarah was saying. 'Just turned thirty, I think. He was doing his clinical sciences while Martyn was a house officer, but they got to know each other and became great friends. One of Nick's special interests is thoracic medicine. That's going to be very useful here.'

Jessica felt her mouth becoming increasingly dry. Nick? Here? She moistened her lips faintly with the tip of her tongue. A light beading of perspiration had broken out on her brow and she rubbed at it with her fingertips, alarmed by the overwhelming surge of feelings that the mere mention of his name had aroused in her.

Get a grip, she told herself. It might not be him. . . But if it is. . .what then? How would she cope, seeing him, working with him every day? She closed her eyes briefly. It had been so hard, this past year, so painful trying to forget, trying to push him from her mind and get on with simply living each day as it came. How was she going to deal with this now, coming so abruptly face to face with the past?

'Ouch, ouch, ouch!' Daniel shouted, putting on a wounded tone as he pushed his finger into the soft mouth of the toy, and from the doorway a deep male voice enquired calmly, 'And what's happening here? Am I walking into the middle of a battlefield?'

'He's biting my finger,' Daniel said, waving the dinosaur in the air under the nose of the man who bent his tall, grey-suited figure towards him. 'See?'

'There's enough there to feed him up for the week, I should think,' the man said, feeling Daniel's chubby digit with long, competent fingers. 'Can you manage with just four fingers on that hand? You didn't need that one for anything, did you?'

Daniel looked at him and giggled. '*Silly*,' he said.

The man grinned, straightening up and turning towards the two women, and Jessica felt as though her heart had flipped right over, felt a flood of heat race through her body as her gaze took in the long, lean frame and the familiar, handsome features.

It *was* him. She felt so unprepared, seeing him again like this. The shock was almost more than she could take, and it was all she could do not to sway on the spot, her head was swimming so much.

He looked exactly as she remembered him, but of course it had only been just a year and a few months since they had parted company. It wasn't likely that he would have changed very much. There were perhaps one or two faint lines around his eyes, and a thin, almost imperceptible vertical cleft beginning in the smooth sweep of his brow that hadn't been there before. His hair, though, was still that same intense black, springy and vital, thick and lustrous. She still had that same compulsion to run her fingers through it, feel the crackle of static, but she curled her hands instead into the fabric of her skirt.

Sarah said, 'You haven't met Jessica yet, have you, Nick? She's our practice nurse. She's been away on a course—another one to add to her armoury. . .you wouldn't believe the number of skills this girl has under her belt; she's a real asset to the centre. She's only been with us since last April, but we've learned enough to know that we wouldn't want to be without her.'

Nick's glance moved over Jessica, but there was no welcoming smile for her. The grey eyes that had smiled for Daniel and Sarah were now cool, impassive, the cleanly sculpted lines of his face carefully controlled.

'We've met,' he said.

'You have?' Sarah's eyes were wide with surprise. 'I had no idea. How is it that you two know each other, then?'

'Jessica and I have worked together. On the paediatric ward at the Royal.'

'Well, that is good news,' Sarah remarked with satisfaction. 'But that must have been some time ago, mustn't it? How long has it been since you were at the Royal, Nick?'

'About three years. I was doing my last stint of GP training.'

'And, round about then, Jessica must have been working for her sick-children's nurse certificate,' Sarah mused, glancing from one to the other. 'Am I right?'

Jessica nodded. 'That's right.'

Sarah smiled. 'And after that I know you were both involved in lots of other things. Nick with his GP and locum work, and you went on later to do that specialised course in paediatric renal nursing, didn't you? You both seem to have packed so much into the last few years—I can imagine there must be a lot you want to talk about.' She picked up her bag and briefcase from the table. 'And I'd better leave you to it, and get on my way. I must go and acquaint myself with my list of morning calls. As soon as I've worked out my route, I can drop Daniel off at the nursery.'

Shepherding Daniel towards the door, she turned and added, 'I'm glad you're back, Jessica. Martyn will be, too. Which reminds me, I must have a word with you about the wedding some time. You did know we were planning to tie the knot? The news seems to have spread around here like wildfire.'

Jessica nodded. 'I heard—I'm really happy for you, Sarah; we all thought it was only a matter of time, anyway.'

Sarah's mouth quirked. 'So I've been told. I wondered how you would feel about being a bridesmaid? Think about it, and we'll talk later. Nick's promised to be Martyn's best man.

Anyway, I must go or I'll be late. See you both.'

The silence seemed to echo around the room after she had gone. Left alone with Nick, Jessica felt all her misgivings return with a rush. She was strangely tongue-tied now, miserably uncertain as to how he was taking the discovery of finding her here. Or had he already known that she would be working in the practice? Somehow, glancing at his taut features, she didn't think so.

When he spoke his tone was oddly remote. 'She seems to think very highly of you. You've certainly made a niche for yourself here.'

She found her voice at last, though it came out dry and edged with huskiness. 'Do you have any objection to that?'

He shrugged. 'It's a complication I could have done without, but your position here is a fact, as is mine, and there's nothing to be done about it now. I was surprised, I admit. I thought you had a career all mapped out in hospital nursing, and this is the last place I'd have expected to find you.' The grey eyes lanced her flesh like cold steel. 'Still, I've no doubt we'll find a way to work together like civilized people. We have to; after all, we have little choice.'

She tried not to flinch under that cold gaze. His contempt for her was all too plain. The intervening year had done nothing to mute the bitterness he felt towards her, and any hopes she might secretly have nurtured, that they could at least in the end come to share a tentative friendship, withered and died on the spot. Inside her, the wound of parting that had subsided over the past months to a dull ache throbbed into sharp, pulsing life.

It had been foolish to expect anything more. The times they had spent together in love and laughter were past now, gone forever, and the dream she had once cherished, of sharing her life with this man, had turned to ashes, leaving only an acrid taste in her mouth and the sting of sharp tears behind her eyes.

'I'm sure you're right,' she managed in a stilted fashion. 'We're both professionals, aren't we? There's no reason why we shouldn't put the past behind us and get on with the job in hand, is there?'

She wasn't going to go into the whys and wherefores of her change in direction from hospital nursing to her situation now. It wasn't a decision she had taken lightly, and her feelings were still too raw for her to lay them open to discussion with anyone else, least of all with Nick. He would simply have to accept the way things were.

'No reason at all,' he said briskly, glancing at the clock on the wall. 'And I must make a start—I have a full surgery ahead of me. What's on your agenda—is it the bloods clinic this morning?'

'It is. I'd better go along to the treatment-room and start getting things ready.'

She looked at him as he turned away, taking in the carved strength of his features, the firmly moulded mouth, the challenging thrust of his jaw. He, of course, had always known where he was going. From the moment he had set out to study medicine he had had his goal before him. He was going to work as a GP. He had known with certainty what it was that he wanted out of life and he was set fair to achieve his every ambition.

At one time Jessica had been part of all that. She had been swept along with him, woven into the close-knit fabric of his life. But not any more.

She had dissolved those threads of her own volition, and no matter how much it hurt, no matter how much she might wish things could have been different, there was no going back now. The days of fun and laughter were well and truly behind her.

## CHAPTER TWO

THERE wasn't a lot to organise for the morning clinic, since her stand-in had ensured everything was neatly in its place, but once she was alone Jessica was glad of the chance to busy herself with the trolley, gathering up the tourniquet and syringes, checking the phials were in order.

She wasn't going to think about Nick. She was going to concentrate her mind on her work, on seeing to her patients to the best of her ability. Things had turned out badly, and the months ahead promised to be strewn with pitfalls of one kind or another, but somehow she had to cope. The last thing she needed was to keep turning events over in her mind. She wouldn't, she couldn't, let Nick's presence here faze her.

It was still only a quarter of an hour before nine o'clock, but a quick glance around the small waiting area outside the treatment-room showed that it was already filled to capacity with people waiting to be seen.

She looked down at her list of names and called the first patient.

'Mrs Simpson?'

A slender brunette in her late twenties stood up carefully and made her way slowly towards her. Jessica recognised the young arthritic, noticing that she looked rather pale, and that her movements were stiff. 'Mandy, isn't it? Would you like to come through?'

She closed the door behind the woman and indicated a grey leather-covered chair.

'Put your coat on the couch there, and take a seat,' she invited with a smile. 'Do you have your form with you from the hospital? How are you feeling today?'

'I'm a bit sore,' Mandy admitted, passing over the form, and pushing back the sleeve of her jumper. 'It's too early in the morning for me yet. It takes me a couple of hours to get going properly.'

'I think you're doing amazingly well,' Jessica told her, checking the form to see what tests were needed. 'Plasma viscosity. . .platelets. . . full blood count,' she murmured, reaching for two small bottles. 'You've two young children to see to, haven't you? They must be quite a handful.'

'They're full of beans,' Mandy smiled. 'But thankfully they're both at the infant school, so I can do a bit of part-time work to help out with funds, without having to feel guilty about leaving them.'

Jessica inspected the veins in Mandy's bared arm. 'That one looks as if it will do nicely,' she said, placing a pillow under the limb for support. That done, she slid the tourniquet over Mandy's upper arm and fastened it carefully. 'How are you coping with the job these days? You're a typist, aren't you?'

'That's right. Things are much better than they were a few months ago. The rheumatologist at the hospital injected my shoulders, and that made me feel a lot better. He put me on some different tablets and they do seem to be bringing things under control. It's a slow business, though.'

'Just so long as we get there in the end,' Jessica said, quickly swabbing the skin around the inner elbow and inserting the needle into the vein. 'That's what matters.' She checked the syringe. 'Two small phials are all we need today,' she murmured. 'I expect you're beginning to get used to these, aren't you? How often do you have these tests now?'

'Once a month. They don't really bother me too much, you know.'

'That's good,' Jessica grinned. 'Some people turn green at the sight of a needle.'

'Not me,' Mandy told her. 'At least I'm glad I can have them done here, rather than having to trek over to the hospital every time. This way I don't lose too much time off work.'

Jessica released the tourniquet and removed the needle. 'All done. Just press this pad firmly on the skin for a minute, will you, while I write out the labels for the bottles?'

When she had finished she put the labelled phials to one side with the form, to be sent to the hospital laboratory, then turned back to her patient.

'That looks fine,' she said, removing the pad briefly and peering at the site. 'I'll pop a dressing on it for you. You can take it off once you get home.'

'Thanks,' Mandy said, getting to her feet a moment later.

'See you next month,' Jessica smiled. 'You take care, now.'

She watched her leave the room and felt real sympathy for the young woman, though it was a relief to see her looking a little better than she had done some time ago. The consultant at the hospital was a good man, by all accounts, so at least she was in safe hands.

'Can I interrupt you before you bring in your next patient?' Sarah asked, peering round the doorway with Daniel in tow. 'I need some sharps for my bag, and some insulin. . .and some paper for Daniel to draw on for a minute or two wouldn't go amiss. Just while I sort myself out.'

'Of course. Help yourself,' Jessica told her, reaching for a notepad and felt pens from the table and handing them over to Daniel before he could embark on a keen, hands-on survey of everything in the room. 'Do you have many calls to make this morning?'

'Half a dozen. Nothing desperately urgent, though, from the looks of things. You can bet those kind of calls will come when the floods are out hereabouts, or when the ground's covered in snow and ice.'

'Isn't that the way?' Jessica agreed.

'At least the car's not played up for a while,' Sarah murmured, pushing things into her brief-case, 'not since its last service, anyway. Nick reckons he used to drive an old Ford and he dreaded seeing snow on the ground, because you could guarantee he would have trouble getting it started those mornings. As soon as he could after that bad winter he changed it. Of course, I expect you already know that—I was forgetting, it must have been round about the time you worked together.'

'Yes,' Jessica said thoughtfully, remembering. 'The snow seemed to lie around for weeks. I didn't have the same problem as Nick, though. I used to walk to work in those days. I didn't live far from the hospital then, but the snow came up over my boots, and you could bet that by the time I arrived on the ward my feet would be icy and wet.' Her mouth made a little quirk. 'In fact, the first time Nick saw me I was sitting in the sluice-room with a towel wrapped around my toes, muttering to myself about the foul British climate. I felt a bit of an idiot, really.'

'I shouldn't imagine Nick would bother about something like that,' Sarah murmured, pulling open a cupboard door and scanning the shelves inside. 'What did he say to you?'

'He was a bit concerned about something,' Jessica recalled. 'He'd come on the ward to examine a toddler about fourteen months old—he'd been admitted with a chest infection. He said to me, "Do you think you could come and give me a hand? I want to examine the little chap. It looks as though something very odd's happened. His leg seems to have swollen enormously, and I've never seen anything quite like it. I need you to hold him while I ease his trousers off him and check it over properly."'

She paused a moment as Daniel held up his picture for the two women to admire, then went on, 'I was so worried, because no one had mentioned this new development to me, and I hadn't noticed anything myself. I pushed my feet into my shoes and went after him as fast as I could.'

'What was it?' Sarah asked, puzzled, and Jessica's mouth gave a faint twitch.

'The diagnosis was quite simple, really. The tab on his nappy had come adrift, and the whole thing had slipped down around one leg. You might say it was an acute case of nappyitis.'

Sarah laughed. 'I'd like to have seen that. I'd like to have seen Nick's face.'

'It was a picture.' The reminiscence brought a sudden, unexpected bright sheen to her eyes, and she blinked quickly, hoping that Sarah would see nothing amiss. 'Is there anything else you need?' she asked, changing the subject. 'Anything I can get for you?'

'Nothing, thanks; I'm all finished. We'll be on our way and leave you to get on.'

Left alone once more, Jessica worked her way through the rest of her list in smooth order, thankful that there were no problems to slow her progress this morning. Seeing Nick Tyler first thing had been quite enough of a shock to her system, and more than enough to send her off balance for the rest of the day. Just thinking about him was proving hazardous.

There were no faints among her patients, though, no nausea or bleeding, and the small waiting-room emptied gradually, with only one other interruption, coming from Dr Castlemaine, the second senior partner.

'Would you do a pinprick test on one of my patients?' he asked quietly. 'I suspect she's a bit anaemic and I'll need to prescribe iron.'

'No problem,' Jessica said. She liked James Castlemaine. He was usually even-tempered, easy to get along with. He had a wife and two young sons, and he was invariably in a good humour. 'Send her along and I'll do it right now.'

The procedure was quick and simple to carry out, and the patient left after a few minutes to go back to James's room.

Jessica finished the bloods, then attended to various people who presented themselves at intervals with dressings to be changed, or stitches to be removed.

Things quietened down at last, and she wondered whether she ought to make a start putting her notes on computer, or whether maybe she'd do better having a coffee first. Coffee, she decided, reaching for the pot.

As usual, the tiny island of peace was short-lived. She'd scarcely finished pouring the hot liquid into her cup, when Nick walked into the room. He looked around, his eyes taking in every detail of his surroundings.

'Did you want something?' Jessica asked. She pushed her cup to one side and stood up as he came towards her. It gave her more of a feeling of being on a level with him, though that was always something they'd laughed about in the past. At five feet three, she'd always had to look up to him, conscious of the fact that the top of her head barely reached his chin. It had never mattered before. She'd worn high heels whenever she was off duty, and she'd told him it was so he couldn't dominate her with his height. In truth, she liked the look of slender heels—they made her legs seem more shapely—and Nick had said he had a thing about her legs.

The thoughts flitted inconsequentially through her mind as he approached the desk. He was long and lithe, his body frame strongly muscled, the broad shoulders beneath his grey jacket infinitely capable.

A faint heat crept over her cheek bones. At one time she'd have rested a hand against his chest and he'd have held her close to him, and she couldn't help wishing that things might be the same again, but of course that could never be. She had destroyed what had been between them, she'd done it deliberately, with premeditation, but she'd had no choice, and no one on earth could know how much that had cost her.

'I need you to do a blood-cholesterol check for me,' he said, 'on Jim Matthieson.'

'OK. Though it's a bit late on in the day—it should be a fasting test,' she murmured. 'Has he had anything to eat or drink in the last few hours?'

'No, he was late getting here this morning, but he's followed instructions. I want you to sort out a diet sheet for him, too. He had a heart attack a while back and we have to get him on the road to recovery. He doesn't seem to be responding as well as I'd like.' Turning around, he raised his voice a notch and called to a man who hovered in the doorway, 'Come on in, Jim, there's no need to hang back there; we don't bite, I promise.'

'Are you sure?' The elderly man who stepped inside the room ran a hand through his white hair and looked a trifle sheepish. His glance went to the walls, adorned with pictures drawn by children from the local primary school. 'With all these portraits of Dracula around, you might forgive me for wondering.'

Nick chuckled. 'We do have other methods. Don't worry, I'm sure Nurse Reid here will look after you. Take a seat while she gets things ready. I'll go and find the appropriate form.'

He moved off in the direction of the filing cabinet just as Jessica started towards the trolley, and his arm brushed against her, solid muscle colliding with soft flesh.

He sprang back on the instant as though he had been stung, while Jessica stayed rooted to the spot, every nerve fibre she possessed startled into tingling, vibrant response.

Nick muttered something incomprehensible under his breath, then yanked open the drawer of the filing cabinet with undue force. Jessica waited for the clamour of her pulse to die down before taking refuge in seeing to her patient.

Thankfully she saw that he had turned to study the pictures once more, and had probably noticed nothing untoward.

'Hello, Jim,' she greeted him. 'Come and sit down. It's good to see you up and about again. How are things? Are you keeping well wrapped up against this cold weather we're having?'

'Aye, it's cold all right. Cuts through me like a knife some days. It takes me all my time to get from the house to the newsagent then, and that's not much distance.' He paused to gather his breath. 'Makes me want to stick around the house. Then I see everything that needs doing in the garden and I have to go out and make an effort. It is an effort, too, sometimes.' He trailed off, sounding thoroughly fed up.

Jessica picked up the tourniquet. 'You've had blood taken before, haven't you?' she asked.

He nodded. 'Go on and do it. I shan't look, though.'

She smiled at his expression. 'Turn your head away, then.' He did as she suggested, and as she took the sample she said thoughtfully, 'You love your garden, don't you? Weren't they your potatoes that took first prize in the autumn fayre?'

'You saw them?' His voice took on a brighter note. 'Beauties, they were. I had caulis too, big as that bowl over there, and creamy as you wouldn't believe.'

'Oh, I would,' Jessica told him, finishing the task and placing a dressing on his arm. 'You used to spend hours in that garden, I know.' She glanced at him, noting his drawn, grey features. Nick was right; he didn't look as though he was recovering as well as they could have hoped for. 'You've not been out there digging, have you?'

'I've had to try and do something,' he said defensively. 'The ground needs turning, it needs to be got ready for the spring planting, and I haven't been able to get at it up till now, with being out of sorts, and all.'

She looked at him quizzically. 'So you've been out there, struggling, and making yourself ill?'

His chin jutted. 'They said I should exercise; the doctor at the hospital said it was important. I'm only following orders.'

Jessica laid a gentle hand on his shoulder. 'There's exercise, my love, and, then again, there's exercise. I don't think the doctor meant you should be out there doing work that would tax a younger man.'

'He said I should go for walks, and I do, but that's a struggle, too. What am I supposed to do, vegetate?'

'I think,' she said, 'you should take things a little more slowly to begin with. Don't, for instance, walk uphill, or against a cold wind. And, for goodness' sake, don't do any digging.'

He opened his mouth to interrupt and she shushed him with an imperious lift of her hand. 'No, listen a minute, I know what you're going to say. You're worried about your produce. . .it isn't just for shows, you sell some of it locally, I know that. What we have to do is to try to think of a way round the situation.' She was quiet for a moment, her brow creased in thought, while Jim's mouth took on a resigned, defeated droop.

'I know,' she said at last with a snap of her fingers. 'What about some of the youth groups round here, the Scouts, for instance, or perhaps some able-bodied person who's unemployed, with time on his hands? I know a few people; I'm sure we could fix something up for you.'

'I don't know about that,' Jim said grumpily, shaking his head. 'I've always had my independence. I wouldn't want to be beholden to anyone.'

'And you won't be. Heavens, Jim, you've helped out enough in the past with all the jamborees and fund-raising events and whatnot. I should imagine they'd all be quite put out if they thought you'd had a problem and not gone to them. Stop being such a stubborn old mule and leave it with me. I'll do some ringing around later on today, and see what can be sorted out.'

'You're a regular bossy boots, missy, did you know that?' Jim muttered, but there was a twinkle in his eye, and Jessica wrinkled her nose at him.

'So I've been told. Now, let me find that diet sheet that Dr Tyler mentioned.'

'No more quick fry-ups, and cut out the boiled eggs, is that it?' Jim said gloomily. 'Next thing you'll be telling me to get a woman in, to cook me some proper meals.'

Jessica looked at him and grinned. 'You said it, not me. Myself, though, I've always believed in equality of the sexes. There's no reason why a man shouldn't cook decently for himself. In fact. . .' her green eyes lit with mischief '. . .they're running classes at the local school—cooking for retired people. . .though of course, who's to say you mightn't meet up there with some nice, homely body who'd like to make you her life's work? Now there's a thought. . . Perhaps I could——'

'Dr Tyler,' Jim said plaintively, 'can't you do something, can't you rescue me from this?'

'Who, me?' Nick said, lifting a dark incredulous brow. He'd been leaning against the filing cabinet, watching them, but now he straightened up. 'You want me to interfere, to get in the way of a determined woman? You must be joking. . .I value my hide far too much to take a risk like that.'

'Pshaw!' Jim pronounced gruffly. 'I can see I'm outnumbered here. Give me the diet sheet and I'll get on my way before she comes up with any more ideas.'

Jessica handed it over. 'I'll be in touch,' she threatened. 'Try to behave yourself in the meantime.'

Nick saw him to the door. 'Come and see me again next week, Jim. We should have the results of the blood test by then. And Jessica's quite right, you know. Light exercise is the thing. Walking's ideal, on the straight, when it's not too cold, but no digging, lifting, or pushing heavy loads in the wheelbarrow. Do as she says. Behave yourself.'

'Pshaw!' Jim muttered.

Nick closed the door on his retreating figure, then lounged back against the wood, not moving, but watching Jessica as she dealt with forms and phials.

The silent scrutiny made her feel oddly uncomfortable. 'What?' she said, her voice faintly challenging. 'You're staring, Nick.'

'Was I?' He pushed himself away from the door. 'You handled him well. I'd no idea he was driving himself like that. I suppose I just haven't been here long enough to get to know people properly yet.'

'It'll come soon enough, I expect.' She pushed the trolley to one side. 'Is that it for the morning? Is your surgery finished?'

'It appears to be, but there's a meeting scheduled for later on.' His glance went to the table. 'Your coffee's cold.'

She sighed. 'It usually is.'

He picked up a pen from the desk, toying with it, and her gaze followed his movements, drinking in the sweep of those long, capable fingers. He had a surgeon's hands, she had told him once, they were sure and dextrous, but he had never had any inclination towards that sphere.

He said casually, 'Do you like working here? It's very different from what you're used to. I never pictured you doing anything other than working with children.'

A chill crept into her bones. 'I like it well enough,' she answered carefully. 'There's always room for change in anyone's life.'

His gaze met hers steadily. 'Yes. That's one lesson I learned by heart.' Tossing the pen to one side, he said calmly enough, 'And. . .talking of change. . .how are things with you and Matthew these days?'

She blinked, her throat constricting in a sudden spasm. 'Matthew?' she echoed huskily.

'Matthew,' he repeated, his tone cynical now, his mouth twisting at her startled prevarication. 'You *are* still seeing him, aren't you? He *was* the man you broke our engagement over, after all.'

# CHAPTER THREE

'I. . . Yes. . .' she said hesitantly. 'I'm still seeing him.'

It wasn't quite a lie, but it was better than telling the full truth in the long run. It was better that Nick went on thinking that the two of them were involved, even though it was costing her dearly to deceive him this way.

'Are you two still living together?' he probed bluntly. 'I know you've both moved house in the last year.'

The stark question threw her off balance for a moment, but she recovered herself enough to counter, 'We were never living together, as you put it. You know that well enough, Nick. You're being deliberately provocative.'

'Am I?' His mouth set in a hard, uncompromising line.

'You know you are.'

It had always been a bone of contention between them, the fact that she'd moved from the high-rise nurses' accommodation to share a house with two of her friends. The house had been converted into flats, with the girls occupying the ground floor, while Matthew and Steve had taken over the upper storey. Nick had never liked the set-up there.

She said, 'It was an ideal solution for all of us. The rents we'd been paying were far too high.

When Sophie's father offered Tracey and me the chance to move into his property for a nominal rent we jumped at it. You could hardly have expected us to do anything else, considering our circumstances. None of us felt we were being overpaid and able to afford much else. You always did make more of that than there was. It was purely by chance that the upstairs flat was taken by men. It could just as easily have been taken by women. You were jealous, right from the start.'

'Not exactly, though I should have had good reason, as it turned out,' he remarked drily. 'When you lived in the nurses' quarters near the hospital there was no problem. We went around together, and got to know each other, and the future looked rosy for both of us. It was only when you moved house that things started to go wrong, for no reason at all that I could see. Except that you were seeing Matthew every day, getting closer to him. What was I supposed to think?'

She could understand how it had looked to him. But even though her mind screamed out to her to say, No, you're wrong, you're completely wrong, it was the one thing she couldn't do, because then he would demand to know the real reason why everything had gone so terribly awry.

'I never set out to hurt you,' she said quietly. 'Things were very confused for me then.'

'And now everything's crystal-clear,' he acknowledged, his tone sardonic. 'You know exactly what you're doing.' He picked up a rubber stamp from the table and examined it briefly before replacing it next to the ink pad. 'So, where are you living now? Near here, by all accounts.'

'Yes,' she said, relieved to be on safer ground. 'I wanted something fairly close, and when a flat became vacant at Sedgeley I went after it right away. It's over the local supermarket. It's modern, the building's only about fifteen or so years old, and the rooms are a reasonable size, so there's lots of space.'

'Over the supermarket?' he repeated. 'I thought you always longed for your own house with a garden you could lose yourself in?'

'Well, that's true enough,' she agreed. 'But there wasn't exactly a choice of properties to be rented round here. It's unfortunate there's no garden, but at least there's a flat roof, a bit like a terrace, and I can sit out there in the summer and look out over the surrounding area. It isn't too bad, really. I planted some tubs up there to add a bit of colour. There are houses round about, and some common land opposite, with a brook and lots of greenery, and over the other side there are fields. The local air ballooning club often set out from there. I think they race each other, or something along those lines. I get a bird's-eye view, so to speak.'

'And Matthew? Is he there with you?'

Her mouth stiffened a little. Nick had always been persistent in ferreting out information. It had been a nightmare when she'd broken off the engagement, trying to keep her true feelings hidden from him.

'I don't believe in living together,' she muttered. 'I'm old-fashioned that way, I guess. No,

Matthew has his own place now, but he wanted to stay the other end of town to be reasonably close to the hospital.'

Nick looked at her consideringly. 'He still works there?'

'Oh, yes. He'll make the consultant grade one day, I'm sure. He works very hard, and he studies for all the specialist exams. Actually, he tutored part of the course I went on. He showed everyone how to use the different types of inhalers and nebulisers, and answered questions on procedures.' She trailed off, conscious that she was babbling, but hoping that she had succeeded in throwing him off course. His questions were getting much too close for comfort.

'How convenient for you both. I'm sure you must have passed with flying colours.'

She sent him a withering glance. 'Sarcasm, they say, is the lowest form of wit.'

'I wasn't aiming to be funny. As to the course, I imagine you already knew how to cope with asthmatics.'

'Well, yes, mostly. It was a health-promotion course really, and the asthma section was only one of several. It was aimed at general practices. It's always wise to keep up to date. You'd be the first to say so.'

'That's true enough. I still think you're wasting your qualifications by working here, though. You're a skilled children's nurse.' His gaze was direct, searching. 'It was what you trained to be, and yet you seem to have thrown all that overboard to come here.'

'I don't want to talk about that,' she said

abruptly. 'I made my decision, and that's an end to it.'

Shifting her glance to the table, she gathered up the various pieces of paper that held her morning's notes, and pushed them into a file. Laying it down by the computer, she asked in a lighter tone, 'So what happened to your work in Nottingham? Didn't it turn out as you hoped, or was Martyn's offer of a job here so tempting that you couldn't resist?'

'I enjoyed the work well enough. I was sharing a flat with my cousin Chris, and commuting back here to see the family about once a month. I found I missed them. I hadn't expected to, and life was certainly full enough with Chris dragging me from one social event to another—there were times when I didn't think there were enough hours in the day. . .'

Jessica hadn't been expecting the sharp stab of anguish that assailed her just then. It came so suddenly, out of nowhere, shattering her with its intensity. Of course he would have made a life for himself without her. There would be new places, new friends. . .other women. . . The pain came again, turning her stomach in sickly revolt.

'But I suppose living around here for all these years has spoiled me for anywhere else,' Nick was saying. 'The Tylers are a boisterous brood, opinionated and downright nosy at times, but I realised that, for all their faults, I like having them around. I like hearing how Robert's research is going, and it gives me a buzz to see Chloe and Adam growing up, bit by bit, and to watch them learn something new each week.'

He had always been good with children. More often than not, her visits to his parents' home with Nick had been filled with the sound of babies and toddlers, his brother's offspring, or his cousin's. She'd watched him play games with them and mend their toys. He'd given them so much love and affection.

He would make a wonderful father one day; she had never doubted that. He had said he wanted children of his own. Children that they would make together. . . Just thinking about it brought a lump to her throat, and she averted her gaze from him now, taking refuge in tidying the surface of the table.

They'd celebrated their engagement in the spring, and they'd planned to marry the following Christmas. She remembered how full of excitement they'd been, searching for a house of their own, a big house, Nick said, one that they would fill with children. . .

'You've always been a very close family, haven't you?' she said after a while, when she had recovered herself a little. She understood how he felt about them. Her own family was much smaller than his, but even so there was a lot of love, a lot of caring. 'They're always interested in what you're doing, what your plans are.'

'Too much that way, sometimes. Especially Claire, but I suppose her heart's in the right place, for all that. She might be five years younger than me, but you wouldn't think so to hear her talk. She's always telling me how I should be going about things.'

'It must be the midwifery training,' Jessica

mused. 'She's used to taking command. You could say that of all your family, though. They've mostly chosen the medical profession, haven't they?'

'Except Jennifer, but even she writes medical articles from time to time.'

Jennifer was the youngest, at twenty-two, just a couple of years younger than Jessica, and starting a career in journalism.

'So,' Jessica said, 'you decided to come back here.'

'When the opportunity arose, yes. I liked the sound of this practice, and I was glad of the chance to work with Martyn. We always got on well together.' He glanced at the clock on the wall. 'Speaking of whom, our meeting starts in five minutes.'

He walked towards the door then, adding, 'Thanks again, for your help with Jim Matthieson. Now I've a bit more idea what's behind his lack of progress, I shall know how to proceed from here on. Perhaps we could get a few more copies of those diet sheets, by the way. We seem to be running rather low.'

He was back to his usual brisk efficiency, his mind returning to work with the ease of one who could switch on and off in a matter of moments.

Jessica didn't find it quite so simple to do that. Now she nodded, making a note on her pad about the diet sheets, and then she was alone again, and the treatment-room seemed stark and clinical, bereft of warmth.

She had hoped that in the end, in the long term, she could resign herself to the decision she had made over a year ago. She had thought she might, sooner or later, come to accept the bleak emptiness that was to remain forever part of her life, but now the terrible finality of it cloaked her once more, making everything seem dark and drab, as though the sun had weakened and died away.

Thinking back, she remembered that other time when the world had seemed to close in on her, crowding her with eventualities she didn't want to face.

It had been late autumn when Nick had gone away on a month's course, just a few weeks before their wedding would have taken place. She hadn't been feeling well, and Nick might have wondered at her dull manner, but he'd put it down to her usual monthly problem, and offered sympathy and support.

'You'll feel better in a few days,' he'd said. 'You usually do. Try soaking in a warm bath to relax your muscles. That sometimes helps, doesn't it?'

She'd never told him the true cause of those monthly problems, and he'd assumed it was run-of-the-mill, the kind of thing most women got at some time or another, some more than most.

He'd gone away, and this time she'd known she had to go back to her doctor. A grimace twisted her lips as she remembered.

'It's the same problem as before,' he'd said. 'Endometriosis. But you know that, don't you? I'll refer you to the hospital.'

She'd known, and she'd pushed it to the back of her mind. The treatment she'd had over the years hadn't helped. Perhaps she'd been unlucky. Her system had reacted badly to the tablets she'd been given, there had been unwelcome side effects, and she'd had to abandon them.

She'd learned to cope, nevertheless. Now, though, as the wedding date had drawn nearer, she was finding that she needed answers to questions that refused to stay buried any longer.

She'd known a fair amount about endometriosis, and she'd known that there could be problems for her in her marriage. It had suddenly become desperately important to know if there was anything more that could be done, what her chances would be of conceiving the children that Nick wanted.

'It's difficult to say,' the specialist had mused. 'The adhesions are fairly extensive in your case, and certainly both ovaries are involved. Of course, an operation might help relieve the symptoms, but then we could be left with the problem of scar tissue. The outcome is never easy to predict. . .it's true to say that fertility might be a problem for you, but you should always try to look on the bright side, you know. You're still a young woman, and not even married yet; you have years ahead of you before you need start to worry.'

On the whole, her visit to him hadn't helped. He'd talked about long waiting lists and priorities, and he hadn't been particularly sympathetic to her anxieties. She'd felt as though she'd been left with an 'if, but, and maybe' kind of solution.

He'd advised her to be optimistic, but she'd only had to look at her sister and her aunt to know what the future might hold for her. Both Suzy and Becky had the same condition as she did. It seemed to be a family trait, and neither of the women had been able to conceive the child she longed for. More than a few tears had been shed, and Jessica had grieved along with them, sharing in their unhappiness and in the eventual acceptance of their lot.

Now it had looked as though an indifferent fate was dealing her the same cards, and she'd known she had no choice but to come to terms with what that might mean.

Would it be fair, though, to ask the same of Nick?

She'd thought about it, long and hard, but the fact was she couldn't do that to him. How could she marry him, knowing that she might never be able to give him the family he dreamed of?

Of course, if she'd told him the truth he would probably hurry to say that it didn't matter, he might try to protect her, but she didn't want to live her life feeling that somehow she had let him down. He might come to resent her, might in the end come to blame her for his loss.

When he'd come back from his course she'd told him she was having second thoughts about the wedding. Even now, she could see his stunned expression, and recall how much of a body blow her rejection of him had been.

'You've been feeling ill,' he'd said. 'You're not thinking clearly; it's just wedding nerves, that's all.'

'No,' she'd told him. 'It's more than that—I'm not sure about anything any more. I need time to myself, to think things through. We'll call off the arrangements while there's still time.'

He hadn't taken it well. In fact, he'd refused to believe that she'd meant what she'd said.

And then there'd been that fateful night, when she'd thought she was alone in the house, and Matthew had come home to find her quietly weeping in the living-room. He'd put his arms around her, in an age-old gesture of comfort, soothing her gently. . .and that was how Nick had found them when he'd let himself into the downstairs flat some ten minutes later.

He had drawn his own conclusions, and it had seemed so much simpler, then, to let him go on believing that she and Matthew had had something going. . .

'You should tell him the truth,' Matthew had said later. 'Let him decide for himself what he wants to do, knowing all the facts.'

But she couldn't do that. Nick was a good man, he deserved the best out of life, and she couldn't deny him the chance to find it.

On the day they should have been married she'd gone away to the south coast, to stay with Aunt Becky, and when she'd come back a month later, just a little more in control of herself, she'd discovered that Nick had already left the area.

## CHAPTER FOUR

A FLU epidemic kept all the doctors hard pressed over the next few weeks. There were more than the usual number of call-outs, and Jessica couldn't remember the last time her clinics had been so busy. They were full of frail or elderly people who had been unfortunate enough to fall foul of the icy weather and the treacherous pavements it produced.

She began to wonder whether Nick was avoiding her. She hadn't seen much of him, only brief moments at the beginning or end of surgery, or when he was on his way out to make his morning visits. He rarely stopped to talk to her, other than when it was absolutely necessary where patients were concerned. It was as though he had made up his mind to keep the relationship between them on a strictly professional basis.

She wasn't sure how she felt about that. Nick's method of handling the situation was probably for the best, and she knew she ought to be rational about the whole thing, but it hurt so much to be this close to him, yet at the same time so coldly distant. All she could do was to accept the way things were and be thankful that at least it gave her the chance to get her emotions under control.

If she'd thought February was a bracing month, March showed few signs of being much better. Rain lashed the trees around the centre, and there was still a bitterly cold wind that had her blowing on her fingers to warm them as she walked into Reception to prepare for the morning's clinic.

Martyn Lancaster was going through his post, but he put it to one side as she came in, and went over to the coffee maker.

'Here, drink some of this,' he said, handing her a steaming cup. 'You look as though you need it. It'll stoke you up for the day.'

'You must have read my mind,' she grinned, taking it from him and clasping her fingers thankfully around the bowl. 'I hope it goes down as far as my toes. I think my legs have frozen up.'

His blue eyes lit with wry amusement. 'This cold spell can't go on for much longer. At any rate, it had better improve in the next three weeks, or Sarah will be going up the aisle in wellington boots and a rain mac.'

'That should make the wedding photos a hoot.' She chuckled, then sobered and said, 'Still, in a few weeks' time it could well be beautiful. It will be spring, after all, and you can go off on your honeymoon and forget all about the centre for a while.'

'I'll keep my fingers crossed,' Martyn said. 'At least there shouldn't be too much disruption here while we're away. We'll only be gone for a week, and John Stokes and his wife have said they'll fill in for us.'

'Only a week?' Jessica said mournfully, putting on a crestfallen face. 'You mean we're to have you back so soon?'

'Cheeky madam.' Martyn's brows met in a threatening gesture that was instantly belied by the widening curve of his mouth. 'Actually, Sarah doesn't want to be away from Daniel for any longer than that. We'd planned on taking him along with us, but we were strongly vetoed by the grandparents and Daniel joining forces. He's been promised all manner of treats.'

Jessica laughed. 'I expect he'll be spoiled to bits.'

'Probably. The only way Sarah would even consider leaving him was by making sure that we'll be in touch by phone every day, and that if he shows any signs of being miserable the grandparents will bring him out to join us. It's understandable that she should be concerned. He's had enough change in his short life, losing his father when he was a toddler, and now having me come on the scene.'

'He thinks the world of you.'

'Yes. I'm glad of that.' He went back to the pile of letters he had been studying. 'Time I finished sifting through this lot. Another five minutes and I shall have to make a start on surgery.'

Glancing through the glass windows that blocked in the reception counter, Jessica saw that the waiting-room was already beginning to fill up for the start of the day. Hurriedly she gulped down the last of her coffee, and said, 'Me too. I'd better be off.'

She went to the treatment-room and worked her way steadily through her list of appointments. Wednesday mornings were always a bit of a mixture, but she quite liked that. There were usually a few tetanus jabs, and so forth, to be done first thing, followed by routine urine tests and the occasional ear syringing or wounds that needed dressing.

Sarah put her head round the door part-way through the morning.

'I just want to check Catherine Markham's urine test result,' she said. 'Have you done it yet?'

'Thirty weeks pregnant, is that the one?'

'That's it. Any result?'

'Sugar's high again. Here, take a look.'

Sarah reached for the form. 'Hmm. Still, I think we'll be safe enough keeping to dietary measures.'

'She certainly looked well enough. She said she was feeling fine, just a bit tired.'

Sarah nodded. 'The blood tests were reasonable, so I don't think we need worry too much about diabetes. I'll need to prescribe iron, though. Thanks, Jessica. I'll see you later—I'm in a tearing hurry.'

Jessica returned to her work. She was thoroughly absorbed in it, so involved in what she was doing that she hardly noticed the hours slip by. It was only when Nick walked in as she was finishing off strapping up a sprained wrist that she realised it must be nearing lunchtime.

'How does that feel, Annie?' she asked her patient, trying not to be so hotly aware of Nick looming in the background. 'Is it more comfortable?'

'It's a lot better,' the woman agreed. 'I think I'll go home and take a couple of painkillers. The housework can go hang while I put my feet up for a while.'

'You do that.'

Shutting the door behind her patient, Jessica turned to face Nick. There was a grimness about his features that made her study him watchfully.

'I just came in here to check something on the computer,' he said. 'Mine developed a glitch yesterday, and the man's still working on it.'

'Perhaps it's a good thing you've been on call, then, and not in your room,' she commented lightly. He seemed to be more preoccupied than usual, and she wondered just how many calls he'd had through the night, what problems he'd had to deal with. 'How did it go?' she asked.

'Let's just say I've had better days, and nights,' he answered abruptly. 'Can we bring up the file on Gemma Cresswell?'

'Of course,' she responded, trying not to let herself be thrown by his cool manner. 'Can you give me the address?'

He supplied it and she went over to the computer and pressed a few keys.

'There you are. Gemma. . .' she read off the screen. 'She must be. . .nine years old. . . The usual childhood illnesses, nothing much there. Nothing recent, anyway.'

Nick had come to stand beside her, leaning over her shoulder, one hand firmly clasping the back of her chair, the fingers of his other hand steepled on the table.

Jessica kept her gaze fixed on the screen. She wished she wasn't quite so fiercely aware of him, but she was, and he was so close that if she'd made the slightest movement their bodies would have come into nerve-shattering contact. As it was, the subtle, fresh fragrance of his cologne drifted past her nostrils, the cloth of his dark grey jacket shifted against her arm. His hand, on her chair, brushed her spine, and warmth spread through the fine cotton of her dress, sending odd tremors to course through the length of her body.

'I didn't really expect I would find anything,' he said, a thread of frustration in his voice. 'If she'd been brought into the surgery we might have been able to nip things in the bud.'

She looked up at him then. His eyes were narrowed on the screen, his expression bleak.

'Something's badly wrong, isn't it?'

'I think so. The little girl's very ill. I wondered whether she'd been brought into the surgery at all in the last few weeks but, as you say, there's nothing there.' The frown was back in his eyes. 'The family's just come back from a holiday abroad. The parents say she wasn't too well before they went away, nothing serious, they thought, just a sore throat that they expected would clear up in a few days. She'd been feeling a bit under the weather, but they thought a few weeks in the sun would put her right.'

'But that didn't happen?' she guessed.

'No.' He said it on a harsh breath, a muscle jerking along the line of his jaw. 'She's in a bad way. There are all the signs of glomerulonephritis, and I'm just hoping we're not too late.'

Jessica bit her lip. 'You think there might be renal failure?'

'I'm afraid so,' he agreed, weariness creeping into his voice. 'I had her admitted to hospital late last night. The poor kid looked wretched.'

'The parents must be feeling pretty awful, too.'

'I'm sure they are. We'll just have to wait and see what happens. Let's hope she responds to treatment.'

He looked so drained all at once. A flood of tenderness welled up inside her, and she wished she could have put her arms around him and held him to her.

'You look all in,' she said gently, 'you must have been up all night. Have you finished your calls? If you have, you really should go home and try to get some rest, you know. Relax, and try not to worry. You've done all you can for now.'

'Such concern for my welfare,' he mocked, his glance moving over her, his eyes darkening to a smoky grey-blue. 'What are you—my ministering angel? To do the job properly, you'd at least have to join me there.'

His expression was unfathomable, but somehow she didn't think his comment had been entirely superficial. She floundered, lost somewhere between longing and despair, knowing full well that if she threw caution to the winds and took up his casually tossed challenge she would only be embarking on a course to self-destruction.

'The thought hadn't crossed my mind,' she countered. 'I know that you're perfectly capable of taking care of yourself. Besides,' her glance went around the room, skimming over piles of forms laid to one side, 'as you can see, I'm up to my eyes in work.'

'If you say so,' he drawled, his mouth making a mobile twist. 'I shouldn't want to tread on Matthew's toes, after all. Even though he didn't grant me the same consideration. But then, he probably had due cause to act as he did. He must have received plenty of encouragement along the way.'

Jessica sucked in her breath. She might have answered, but just as she opened her mouth a knock sounded on the treatment-room door and it was flung open suddenly.

A worried-looking receptionist glanced from one to the other, then back to Nick.

'Thank goodness you're here, Dr Tyler,' she said hurriedly. 'We've an emergency out in the waiting-room. A little boy, Lewis Reynolds. His mother's just brought him in as he seems to be having a bad asthma attack. She's in a bit of a state. . .panic, you know. Will you see him? Shall I bring him in here?'

'Of course. I'll go with you to fetch him. We'll try to keep him as calm as possible—the mother, too.'

Jessica shot into action, setting up the nebulizer and checking through the cupboard for supplies of Ventolin and Bricanyl. Just to be completely prepared, she reached to a lower shelf and pulled out Sammy the sock puppet, tucking him into her belt.

By the time Mrs Reynolds appeared in the room a moment or two later she had the child's notes on screen, and she was able to turn to the woman and her small son and give them her full attention.

'Sit down, Mrs Reynolds,' she urged her, indicating the softly cushioned leather chair. 'Make yourself comfortable, and Lewis can sit on your lap while Dr Tyler examines him.'

The woman looked thoroughly distressed, but

she did as she was bid, comforting the frightened, exhausted child with soothing gestures all the time. The boy's breathing was shallow, and there was a blue tinge to his lips. His eyes were wide and frightened.

Jessica didn't waste any time. She needed to divert him, put him at ease and make him feel that he was safe. Tugging Sammy from her belt, she pulled the red felt puppet over her hand, and wiggled its wide mouth in front of the child.

'My, oh, my,' she said, in a surprised tone, 'Sammy wants to sit on Mummy's knee as well. I wonder if there's room?' She knelt down beside the chair and lifted the squirming puppet, watching the child's reaction.

Lewis managed a faint smile, his eyes brightening a little.

'Yes,' said Jessica. 'I think there's room, don't you? Well, would you believe it? He wants Dr Tyler to look at him as well.'

Nick tweaked the puppet's nose.

'I see Lewis has been having these attacks for some time,' he confirmed, quickly glancing through the notes before looking at the boy's mother. 'When did this latest one start?'

'He's been wheezy for days,' the woman replied as Lewis turned his head to watch the puppet's antics. 'He had a cold and a bit of a cough. I kept hoping it would clear up, but it just got steadily worse. He seems to get every infection going. I gave him his inhaler, but it doesn't seem to have helped this time—it got really bad a couple of hours ago after he'd been out playing; he was really struggling for breath. I feel so guilty, but he couldn't wait to get out after the rain stopped. . .he hates being cooped up. I don't know what to do, he will run about so. . .'

'Five-year-olds usually do,' Nick agreed, smiling at the boy as he carefully examined him. 'I expect the cold air has made his breathing more difficult, but we'll soon put that right. Have you used one of these before, Lewis?' he asked, picking up the nebulizer and showing it to the child.

The boy looked at it warily, shaking his head and then breaking off to gasp for breath.

'Not to worry,' Nick said. 'I'll show you how it works. It should soon help you to feel much better.'

Sammy made a takeover bid for the mask, and Nick tut-tutted.

'*You'll* just have to take your turn,' he addressed it firmly. Miffed, the puppet withdrew, pulling a face at Lewis, who, despite his discomfort, gave a small chuckle.

Nick showed the boy what to do, and asked, 'Do you think you can manage that?'

'Think so,' Lewis agreed cautiously, and at Nick's slight nod Jessica twisted open a capsule of solution and emptied its contents into the reservoir of the nebulizer.

'There you are, sweetheart,' she said, helping the child with the mouthpiece. 'Just breathe in as Dr Tyler showed you, and we'll soon have you right again.'

The boy managed surprisingly well, considering it was his first attempt, and after a few minutes it was clear that he was making headway. His mother looked intensely relieved, though she still listened anxiously to what Nick had to say.

'I think I should see him again tomorrow morning, if you could bring him along to surgery,' he told her. 'Bring his inhaler with you, and I'll check to see that he's using it properly. Then we might also look into having the physiotherapist show him how to keep his lungs clear, and try to prevent any further attacks.'

'I'll see the receptionist now, shall I, and make the appointment? I don't want to risk getting here too late and finding your list is full.'

'Yes—get her to book you a time. If you have any problems before then, just give the centre a ring, and someone will come out to you.'

'Thanks, Doctor.'

She went on her way, buttoning Lewis into his coat and helping him out to Reception. Jessica watched them go, her heart twisting a little as she saw the close affection between mother and son. A closeness she might never experience in her lifetime. . .

It was a knowledge brought home to her every time she was called on to tend young children, and it never got any easier.

She drew in a slow, calming breath. There was no future in dwelling on things that couldn't be. She had to force herself to concentrate, to get back on course.

'Do you think he's been missing the proper dosage with the inhaler?' she asked, now that they were alone once more.

'It's a possibility,' Nick said. 'These things need to be used accurately or the drug isn't inhaled properly and the treatment becomes ineffective.

Then the condition worsens. I've seen it happen so often that I think there might be something to be said for setting up an asthma clinic here, just to make sure that both parents and children know exactly how to handle the equipment and cope with attacks. I'd rather they were familiar with procedures before they have to be used. That way they're much less frightening.' He looked at her consideringly. 'You were marvellous with Lewis. You turned what could have been something threatening into something that he could cope with.'

Her shoulders lifted. 'It always helps to lighten the atmosphere.'

'You did it very well. You know, I think we should put the idea of a clinic to Martyn. We could work together on it. You've all the up-to-date information, and you're a natural with children. What do you think?'

Her mind skittered wildly and she had to struggle for a moment to collect her thoughts. His idea was basically a sound one, and she could see that it would benefit the practice in many ways. She couldn't deny she *was* the obvious choice to help with it, since she had only recently been on a course, but she wasn't at all sure how she felt about working with Nick much more closely than they had done up to now. Her love for him coloured her every thought, it was so deeply a part of her, but it was as impossible now as it had ever been. Her emotions had been precariously balanced these last few weeks, and she didn't know how much longer she could go on like this without breaking down.

'I can see from your expression that you're having reservations,' he said drily. 'Because of me, I suppose? Well, that's unfortunate, but it can't be helped. I know it isn't what you want, but I don't see why we should put our patients at a disadvantage because of our personal preferences. One afternoon a week isn't going to break either of us.'

'I-it does sound like a good idea,' she admitted awkwardly. 'I'm not sure that I'm automatically the best choice to manage it with you, though. There are other nurses within the practice who might have had more experience than I have. Besides, at the moment my workload is pretty well organised around other clinics: minor ops, hypertension, weight reduction——'

'Schedules can be reorganised easily enough,' he said briskly. 'As you say, there are other nurses within the practice, whose time isn't so heavily accounted for. The clinics can be rearranged. As to experience, most of the asthmatics we've been seeing lately are young children, and there's no one here who is more experienced in that area than you.'

'But I've moved away from children's nursing,' she said with a kind of desperation. 'I wanted something different. . .I needed to——'

'You're just making excuses,' he cut in bluntly. 'Trying to find a way out. Why? Because you can't face the thought of working next to me for a few hours a week?' His mouth twisted, his grey eyes narrowing on her. 'Maybe we should meet this thing head on, instead of constantly trying to avoid the issue. We're both too conscious of what we had before. Perhaps the best thing would be to find out if the chemistry is well and truly dead and gone. Then we can put it behind us, once and for all.'

She hadn't known, until then, what was in his mind. But now, as he flicked the 'engaged' sign over the treatment-room door and set the lock, she read his intent well enough.

She backed away as he started towards her. He wanted to prove that there was nothing left between them, that the spark had long since fizzled and died, but she knew that if he touched her, if he held her in his arms she wouldn't be able to keep up the pretence any longer. The flame of love and longing had never stopped burning inside her; all it needed was the slightest touch of his lips on hers to fan it into a leaping, wild conflagration.

She drew in a shaky breath. 'Nick, I don't think this is a good idea. You're not thinking clearly—you haven't had much sleep, you're——'

'I do. I am,' he said firmly. 'My mind is perfectly clear. I've been thinking about this for a long while, and I've decided it's high time my theory was put to the test. What are you afraid of? No one is going to come in here. No one will ever know. . .except you and I. . .'

His arms circled her, even as he spoke, and all at once there was nowhere else for Jessica to retreat to. She had run out of space. The wall was at her back, and Nick's long, muscled frame was powerfully close, wonderfully, heart-breakingly close.

His hand opened, palm flat, on the curve of

her spine, gliding down to rest in the hollow in the small of her back. He drew her against him, pressuring her into the warmth of his body, so that the soft fullness of her breasts was crushed to his chest, and she could feel the heavy thud of his heartbeat through the thin material of his shirt. His other hand moved upwards, his fingers tangling in the silk of her hair, drawing it back off her face, his thumb tilting her chin so that her mouth lifted in readiness for the slow, tantalising brush of his lips.

His kiss was warm and gentle, his mouth caressing hers in a way that was so tinglingly, achingly thorough that it took her breath away. Her lips softened, parted, and clung to his in hungry yearning. It was as though the grief and tension of the past months had dropped away, and this was all she had ever lived for. Her fingers slid beneath his jacket to make a quivering exploration of the broad expanse of his chest, and reached up to curl into the hard, velvet-covered muscles of his shoulders.

She wanted the kiss to go on forever. She wanted all of him, she wanted all that he had to give, and more, she wanted this sweet, intoxicating languor to stay with her throughout the long, empty years that lay ahead, and drive out completely all the pain and heartache.

Her breath shuddered in her lungs. She was yearning for the impossible, behaving like an idiot. If she let this go on there would be no going back. It had to end.

She dragged her mouth away from his. His eyes had been half closed, their depths dark and unfathomable, but when he tried to reach for her once more she shifted in his grasp, and as he stared down at her she could see that the smoking embers of desire were charged with darting flame. His breathing was ragged, and his heartbeat had quickened, matching the erratic tempo of her own. She tried to evade his seeking mouth, and he was suddenly still, watchful, reluctantly letting her succeed. His gaze never left her, and his eyes sparked with a new recognition that brought a betraying warmth to her cheeks.

'Well,' he said at last, his voice thickened, 'that was certainly something of a revelation.'

'Was it?' She tried to appear nonchalant about the whole thing. 'Perhaps you're reading more into it than there was.'

'I don't think so, Jessica.' He studied her heat-flushed features with interest. 'For someone who was so ready to throw away everything we had, you're amazingly responsive.'

'Your imagination's working overtime,' she said, hoping that she sounded dismissive. 'You took me by surprise, that's all. I wasn't expecting you to do anything like that, least of all at work. It's been a long time since there was anything between you and me. Let's leave it at that, shall we?' She took in a gulping breath and rushed on, 'You wanted to prove a point, that we could work together without this flaring up between us. Well, you proved it for me. You kissed me, and it was OK, it was fine, but I'm not going to hanker for more.'

She was lying through her teeth, and she hoped her act was convincing. Nick simply stared at her, narrow-eyed, saying nothing at all, and she hurried on. 'Maybe we *could* give the clinic a try. I dare say we could manage it easily enough, just as long as you promise there'll be no more repeats of what happened today.'

A cynical smile touched his mouth. 'Running scared, Jessica? Perhaps you've discovered that Matthew isn't quite everything you wanted, after all.'

'I—I don't. . .' She stumbled over her words and began again. 'You're not listening to me, Nick. You have to hear what I'm saying. I don't want to talk about Matthew, now or any time. This has nothing whatever to do with Matthew. This is about you and me, and that's all over, Nick. It was over a long time ago, and a kiss for old times' sake isn't going to alter that. We aren't going to resurrect the past. It won't work.'

Lord knows, she might wish it would, but dreams were fragile things, wispy as thistledown.

'I've no intention of resurrecting the past,' he said tersely. 'I'm only interested in the future. As to that, I clearly heard you agree to do the clinic with me, and that is what matters, after all. I'll put the idea to Martyn. By the time he comes back from his honeymoon we could have the thing up and running.'

His tone was purely businesslike, his slate-grey eyes cool. It was what she had wanted, and the shutters were firmly back in place. She told herself it was for the best, it had to be done, but when he had gone from the room she sat down in the chair and willed herself not to weep.

# CHAPTER FIVE

SARAH and Martyn were married a few weeks later. Jessica, as chief bridesmaid, found herself walking from the church with Nick at her side, and it was far more nerve-racking than she could ever have expected.

She kept her gaze straight ahead. Since that day, when he'd kissed her, he'd completely detached himself from her, as though, as far as he was concerned, the incident had never happened.

She wasn't finding it so easy to forget. She was all too aware of his strong presence. Even now, as they followed the bride and groom out into the bright spring day, the faintest brush of his arm was enough to set up a tingling, electric pulse of reaction in hers.

Her vision blurred with a sudden shimmering mist of tears, and she blinked it rapidly away. It was the fierce glow of sunlight that was causing the trouble, that was it; it had nothing to do with Nick and their surroundings, nothing at all.

As soon as they stepped outside the church a triumphant peal of bells started up, and within a matter of moments Martyn and Sarah were surrounded by a crowd of family and friends, laughing and chattering and tossing confetti into the air. It swirled brightly in the faint breeze, landing on Sarah's veil and drifting over Martyn's hair and the shoulders of his jacket.

He smiled and looked at his bride, beautiful in ivory silk, then laid a possessive hand about her waist, and kissed her firmly on the mouth, oblivious to anyone around them. Even the loud accompaniment of cheers didn't break up that kiss.

Daniel looked up at them and screwed up his nose. 'They're always doing that,' he announced, losing interest and turning his attention to his brand-new page-boy outfit. He began to pick at the buttons of his waistcoat. 'Don't want this on,' he said to Jessica.

Jessica tried to pull herself together. 'But you look so smart,' she told him, 'so grown up.'

'Even Benjy's wearing a waistcoat,' Nick put in, bending to admire the teddy bear and stroke its furry tum. 'When you have your pictures taken your mummy will be really proud of you.'

Daniel thought about that. 'OK,' he said, as though he was bestowing a favour.

His grandmother appeared at his side. 'You made an absolutely wonderful page-boy back there in the church,' she told him. 'You did everything just right.' She gave him a hug and kissed his cheek fondly, then held out her hand to him. 'Come on, your grandad's wondering where you've got to. Let's go and stand with him.'

Jessica looked around. Everyone from the health centre was there to see the couple wed, and she could see that there were even bystanders watching from the distant street corner, cheering and waving, with boxes of confetti at the ready, and gifts of horseshoes and beribboned spoons and lucky black cats draped over their arms.

Nick, as best man, gathered them up later and put them to one side with all the wedding presents. They had been set out on a table in the huge marquee that had been hired for the occasion. It was decorated with festoons of peach and silver, picking out the warm shade of silk that the two bridesmaids were wearing, and the delicate furled rosebuds that were part of Sarah's bouquet and made up the bridesmaids' headdresses.

A sumptuous wedding feast had been laid out, and Nick took charge of proceedings as the guests sat down to eat. Jessica didn't think she'd ever seen him looking so good. His dark grey suit was immaculate, expensively cut and tailored, making the most of his broad shoulders and long, muscular legs. Just looking at him made her throat tighten up.

When the speeches were over, and the bride and groom had been toasted in champagne, Nick gave out bouquets of flowers to both sets of parents, and handed a gift-wrapped box to Daniel, whose mouth curved in a smile from ear to ear.

Then Nick raised his glass to the bridesmaids, and Jenny from Casualty went over to him with a rustle of skirts, and smilingly accepted her gift of a gold bracelet. He slipped it on to her wrist, and she kissed him, laughing at something he said before she moved away; and then it was Jessica's turn and she felt her cheeks growing hot as she walked towards him.

He held out a long, narrow box. 'Open it,' he said as she stared down at it, bemused. 'That's what everyone expects you to do.'

She did as she was told, putting aside the

embossed paper to disclose a glinting gold necklace on a bed of black velvet.

'It's beautiful,' she whispered, her fingertips making a hesitant foray over the delicate gold tracery. 'I hadn't expected—I mean, I'd forgotten about this tradition. I feel. . .' She stopped then and took a breath. 'Thank you, Nick.'

'It's my pleasure,' he murmured. 'I always thought you had such a graceful neck, so this seemed an appropriate gift. Shall I fasten it for you, or would you prefer to leave it in its box for now?'

To leave it lying there was out of the question, especially with an eager audience looking on. She shook her head. 'I'll wear it,' she said, lifting her hands to remove the single crystal droplet she was wearing.

He moved around her, sliding the gold circlet around her throat, his fingers resting warmly on her vulnerable nape. A tremor passed along the length of her spine, and she hoped desperately that he hadn't noticed. She hoped, too, that no one in the assembled crowd would see anything amiss, and that they'd simply put the warmth of her cheeks down to the build-up of heat under canvas.

She held her breath until he had fastened the clasp and finally released her.

'Thank you,' she said again, huskily, and would have moved away, except that his hands came out to steady her at the elbows, and his head bent towards her.

'More tradition,' he said, his mouth making a faint twist. His kiss was swift and light, the merest brush of his lips on hers, but it was enough to make her mouth tremble with warm, startled response, and when he released her she was conscious only of a sense of utter deprivation.

It had meant nothing to him, of course, but *she* turned away from him feeling completely dazed, and walked slowly back to her table without knowing quite how she had got there. She wasn't sure how she managed to keep from touching her mouth. Her lips felt swollen, were still prickling with sensation, and for the life of her she didn't know how she was going to get through the rest of the afternoon.

She did her very best to keep out of his way, but, when the tables were pushed back half an hour or so later and music started up from the stereo system, he came to find her.

'Shall we dance?' he asked, and when she hesitated he added drily, 'It'll look very odd if we don't, you know. We can hardly avoid each other the whole afternoon. People are very quick to put two and two together and it only takes one to start asking questions.'

He was asking her out of formality, not from any desire to rekindle what they had once had. She'd do well to remember that, and not read anything into his actions other than correct wedding etiquette.

'I'd hate to start the tongues wagging,' she said, and went into his waiting arms.

It was like being in heaven and hell at the same time. His body was warm and loose-limbed, he was relaxed, moving slowly in time with the music, and she couldn't think of anything except being with him, so close to him that she could feel the gentle rise and fall of his chest, could feel the faint drift of his breath on her hair.

Everything went out of her head, the time, the place. . .there was only him, and nothing else mattered, except these few snatched moments.

It was over too soon. The tempo changed, and couples disappeared from the dance floor, others moving in to take their place.

Sharon Castlemaine was handing around pieces of wedding cake and James beckoned Nick over to the drinks table.

'Sorry to break things up,' he said with a grin. 'I think you're needed over here. The caterers want a word.'

Jessica came down to earth with a jolt. For what was left of the afternoon she circulated among the guests, making an effort to be smiling and chatty. To all outward appearances she must have looked as though she was enjoying herself, but if anyone had asked her later what she had said and done she would have had absolutely no idea. The time had passed in a complete blur.

Back at the health centre a couple of days later, she checked her list of morning appointments and took a few minutes to restock the racks with advice leaflets. She just had to keep busy. Anything to take her mind off the fact that they were starting the asthma clinic this afternoon.

It wasn't that she didn't want to see Nick. That wasn't it at all, she admitted to herself ruefully. The plain fact was, she was desperate to see him, and be with him any chance that was going. She sighed heavily. It was such a false situation, and knowing that there was no way out, unless she gave in her notice, was making her more and more restless by the day.

Jim Matthieson came in for another cholesterol check, and helped shake her out of her bleak mood. He was looking a lot better, and she told him so.

'You've a bit more colour than you had last time I saw you,' she said with a smile. 'How are things with you? Did the youth group help out with the garden?'

'Do you know, they did a grand job?' he told her. 'Dug and raked, and some of them even want to come back to give a hand with the planting. We might have a couple of real gardeners amongst those lads. I can see them making a career out of it.'

'That's good news, isn't it? Something more than we expected.'

'You're a good lass,' he said, pulling down his shirt sleeve when she had finished, and fastening his cuff. 'Nosy and interfering, but your heart's in the right place.'

'I notice you said that *after* I took your blood,' she laughed, tossing the syringe into the bin. 'You weren't taking any chances, were you?'

'Not likely!'

He went out chuckling to himself, and Jessica sent a quick glance around the waiting-room.

A man was standing by the door looking a bit ill-at-ease, as though he hadn't quite made up his mind whether to stay or go. He had brown hair, showing a touch of grey at the sides, and she thought he must be somewhere around his mid-forties. He was leanly built, and there was an air of veiled anxiety about him that drew her attention.

'Can I help you?' she asked.

'I don't have an appointment,' he said. 'Dr Castlemaine told me to come and get my weight checked while I wait for Reception to deal with my form.'

'Come through to the treatment-room and I'll do it for you,' she told him. 'Just give me a few details first. I don't think I've seen you here before, have I? Are you new to the area, or just one of those patients we don't see very often?'

He gave a wry smile. 'I keep away if I can. I'm far too busy to be coming to the doctor's every five minutes. I work for myself. I'm an electrician—you don't get work by sitting at home twiddling your thumbs. My name's Templeton,' he added as she pulled out her notepad and glanced up at him. 'Richard.'

She jotted it down, and asked casually, 'And what's the form for, Richard? Is it a hospital request?'

He nodded. 'The doc wants me to have an endoscopy. I've had some problems with the stomach just lately. Best check it out, he says.'

Jessica sensed he might have said more, but he didn't, and she went ahead and weighed him without comment.

'Thanks, that's all done,' she murmured. 'You can put your jacket back on now.'

'I've lost a few pounds, I reckon,' he said.

'I keep being sick. Can't keep much down these days.'

'You're probably working too hard,' she guessed. 'Too much stress. Anyway, the endoscopy will help us to find out what's causing the trouble.'

'I'm not sure I like the idea of someone pushing a tube down my throat,' he said ruefully, and Jessica wondered if that was one of the things that was bothering him, but he hadn't liked to say.

'They usually offer you an injection to relax you,' she said. 'And they'll spray your throat with something so that you shouldn't feel it going down. I've seen it done. Believe me, it isn't as bad as it sounds. It shouldn't take many minutes.'

'Let's hope not, anyway.'

He went out looking a bit happier than he had when he'd come in, and Jessica carried on with the rest of her appointments.

It was the time of year when people were planning ahead for holidays, and the vaccination season was showing signs of getting underway. She gave cholera jabs to an Asian father and son who were going to visit relatives back in India for a few weeks, and there was a request for a typhoid jab from a man heading for the Tropics.

'You'd better have some tablets, as well, to stave off malaria,' she told him. 'Start taking them now, and you'll need to keep on taking them for a while after you get back.'

'That's the one thing I hate about these trips,' he said. 'Having to pill-pop for weeks on end.'

'There's no alternative at the moment,' she

murmured sympathetically. 'There is work being done on a vaccine, but it'll probably be some time before it's available.'

She went out at lunchtime for a breath of air, walking down to the small park where the river meandered lazily and trees dipped their branches overhead. She stood for a while on the bridge and looked down at the water. It was peaceful here, watching the wildfowl slipping in and out of the reeds, and she needed these few moments of quiet, away from it all.

When Nick was around her senses went haywire, and it was all too easy for her to lose track of all the sensible decisions she had made.

He came into the centre after lunch looking fit and full of energy, and she saw that his hair was glinting damply as though he'd not long ago showered.

'You've been playing squash with James,' she guessed. 'Was it a good game?'

'Brilliant,' he said, tossing his briefcase on to a chair. 'There's nothing like it for getting the circulation going.'

'That would be before the heart attack, of course?' she queried sweetly. 'I've seen people in action on the court. It always amazes me how they put themselves through that. You and James and Martyn do it regularly, don't you?'

'You should try it some time. We'll have a match one lunchtime—or evening, whenever.'

'Whenever,' she agreed, laughing, then added, tongue-in-cheek, 'Though the only good time for me would be some time on a Friday evening, so I've the whole weekend to recover. . . You go to your parents' most Fridays, don't you?'

His dark eyes glinted. 'You think you're safe? You think I won't keep you to it? Lady, beware. . .' He grinned at her, and the effect was devastating; it melted her limbs and made her stomach do a funny kind of flip that left her breathless.

She couldn't have spoken if her life had depended on it, and instead her mouth gave an odd little quiver before she brought it under control.

Nick looked at her, laughter still in his eyes, but there was something else too, maybe a flicker of curiosity.

'You disappeared on Saturday,' he murmured. 'I looked for you in case you needed a lift home, but you'd already left.'

'I went with James and Sharon,' she explained. 'They had to take the boys to their grandparents', so it seemed easiest to accept a ride with them.' She started to set up the trolley ready for the clinic. 'The wedding went well, didn't it? I thought you did a great job as best man.'

'Well, thanks. It was a lot easier than I expected. The biggest problem was loading all the wedding gifts into the car to take them to Martyn's place.'

'Is that where they'll be living? What will Sarah do about her house?'

'Rent it out, I expect. She doesn't seem keen on selling, with the property market being in such a depressed state.'

'You wouldn't be interested in taking it over, I suppose? I know you're already renting a house. . .but Sarah's would be nearer to the centre.'

He shook his head. 'It isn't worth uprooting all my belongings for something equally temporary. I'm looking for something more fixed.'

'To buy, you mean?' She paused, her fingers stilling on the tubing of the nebulizer. 'Have you had any luck?'

'None so far. I know what I want, but up to now I haven't been able to find it.'

'What exactly are you looking for?' If her voice was a little strained she hoped he hadn't noticed. She made her hands busy again, rearranging the inhalers and finding a place for the bottle of antiseptic.

'Something detached, preferably three or four bedrooms. It's time I put down roots, I think, and I don't want to be moving every five minutes if circumstances change. I'd like a big garden, too—in fact, it's an absolute must. Plenty of room for the kids to run around. The place I'm in now has a pocket-handkerchief lawn, and it's hardly big enough for Robert's brood to toddle about on, let alone wheel trikes around.'

Jessica's throat swelled painfully, and she swallowed hard, clamping down on the sudden rise of tension within her. What had she expected? Nothing had changed. Why should it? Nick had always known what he wanted out of life, and just because Jessica was no longer around to share it with him didn't mean he'd push those wants on to a back burner.

Maybe he already had someone picked out to live with him in this house he was planning on buying. He hadn't talked openly about his love life to anyone at the centre, but that didn't mean that he didn't have one. He was essentially a private man, and everyone knew how rumour could spread around a place like this. He wouldn't want everyone talking.

She said huskily, 'That doesn't seem too tall an order. It's just a question of time, I suppose, before the right house comes on the market.'

'Hmm. I haven't found one with the proper feel to it yet. But you're probably right; I expect something will turn up before too long.'

He glanced at his watch and added briskly, 'We'd better get this clinic started. Who do we have this afternoon? Mostly children, isn't it?'

With something of a miracle she managed to get herself together and reached for her pile of notes. 'They're all children,' she told him. 'Lewis Reynolds is first on the list. I'll bring him in.'

It took her just a moment to fetch the boy and his mother from the waiting-room.

'Hello, Lewis, Mrs Reynolds,' Nick greeted them as they came into the room. He waved a hand towards the chairs opposite. 'Take a seat. And how are things?'

'He seems to be a bit better now that we've made sure that he's using his inhaler properly,' Samantha Reynolds said, 'but there are still times when I think he might need the nebulizer. I'm never sure whether I'm leaving it too late, and I think then perhaps I should have brought him in. I wonder if I should have a nebulizer at home—but I wouldn't be quite sure about when to use it.'

'I think it would be a good idea to have one

on hand,' Nick said, his manner relaxed and easy. 'We can help with arrangements for that. If I show you how to use this peak-flow meter it should give you more of an idea about what treatment is necessary, and when. That way we can make sure we're keeping things under control.'

Jessica picked up a small calibrated plastic tube and passed it to him before turning to the boy and helping him off with his coat.

'We use this to check lung capacity,' Nick said. 'As soon as I've examined Lewis I'll show you how to take a reading, then we can go on from there. Asthma's a very common complaint these days, and once you know how to handle things you'll realise there's usually no need for concern. If there's anything at all you're not sure of, just ask.'

He was remarkably gentle, Jessica thought, watching him with the child. He was such a caring man, not just concerned with physical well-being, but treating people as though they really mattered. It was why she loved him, of course. Just one of the many reasons.

She turned away, pulling in a taut breath and shutting her eyelids on the bright sheen of tears that appeared out of nowhere. She couldn't go on like this; she was a mess. Her emotions were getting in the way of her professionalism and that wouldn't do at all. It had to stop.

Reaching for the child's attendance card, she occupied herself with the routine task of checking details against his notes.

'OK, Lewis, you can put your shirt and jumper back on now,' Nick said. 'As soon as you're dressed we'll have a look at how you're getting on with the inhaler and I'll show you how to use this peak-flow meter.'

Patiently, Nick waited while the boy shrugged on his clothes, then, in a few minutes, went through the various procedures with the child and his mother.

'I'll take Lewis over to the play corner while you talk to Dr Tyler,' Jessica offered when they had finished with the equipment. There was a small child-size table and chair in the corner of the room, and a collection of toys. 'Let's see what we can find here, shall we?' she said.

Mrs Reynolds seemed glad of the chance to question Nick about her uncertainties, and he, in turn, talked with her until he was confident that she fully understood things.

'So, if his peak-flow reading is down by fifty per cent,' she queried after a while, 'I should get him to use the nebulizer, is that right?'

'Certainly. And he may need to use it again four hours later. Keep a record of his peak-flow readings, along with his use of the inhaler and nebulizer, and bring it with you whenever you come into the centre with him.'

Jessica left Lewis engrossed with a toy post-office van and went over to the desk where the cards were stacked.

'It should be quite easy to follow,' she said, passing the record chart to the woman. 'I've filled in today's readings for you. There's a leaflet here, too, just to remind you of everything Dr Tyler has said. And another one that deals with various things that might be factors in bringing on an asthma attack. It takes a bit of detective work, really, but you might be able to pinpoint one or two things that make matters worse. Like pollen, for instance, or pets about the place, or even certain food and drink.'

'That'll be handy to have,' Mrs Reynolds admitted. 'I know we've been through all these things before, but it is difficult to remember everything. I feel a lot better now it's all been explained to me thoroughly. I think I'll be able to cope without worrying quite so much.'

'That's the idea,' Nick said. 'Keep as calm as you can about the whole thing. That's important for both you and the child. And if you have any anxieties at all, anything you want to check up on, just give us a ring.'

'The extension number's noted down on your card,' Jessica pointed out. 'Just phone Reception, and ask them to put you through. I'll pass on any information to Dr Tyler, and if necessary I can arrange for you to see him.'

'I'll do that,' Mrs Reynolds said, putting cards and leaflets into her bag, along with the peak-flow meter. She looked across the room at Lewis. 'Now my only problem is how I'm going to prise him away from that lot!' She smiled affectionately at her son, who carried on playing, oblivious to everything as he pushed cars round and round a wooden garage with accompanying 'brrm' sounds.

'I think it's time Lewis had his Smiley badge,' Jessica said, raising her voice just a little, and he looked up at that, curious. 'Well done, Lewis,' she told him, sticking the sunshine-yellow circle on to the front of his coat. 'You've been a wonderful little patient. Come and see us again, won't you?'

The afternoon moved smoothly on. Nick examined each small patient carefully, giving advice and encouragement where it was needed. He was unfailingly polite to Jessica, and she only had cause to falter once, when they both reached for something at the same time, and she froze as his fingers tangled with hers.

'Sorry,' he said mildly, and stood back to let her do her job. There was no hint in his manner that he thought anything at all about her oversensitised reaction, but just as he turned away her glance meshed with his and she caught the brooding dark glint that was in his eyes.

She bit down on the softness of her lower lip. Watch yourself, she admonished herself silently. The last thing she needed was to provoke his cynicism or, worse still, invite his curiosity.

The last patient went out, clutching a prescription, and Nick leaned back in his chair. His glance skated over Jessica. 'Well, that wasn't so bad, was it?' he drawled. 'I think the clinic's going to be a great success. I'd say we both managed to survive the afternoon more or less intact, wouldn't you?'

There was a lacing of mockery in his tone that made her draw in a sharp breath. 'I hardly expected anything different,' she remarked evenly. She wasn't going to rise to his baiting. It was what he wanted, and she wasn't going to give him the satisfaction. 'If you're through in here, I'll finish clearing up and head for home. I need to stop by the shops and I don't want to be too late.'

'You have plans for this evening?'

'Oh, nothing too special. I mean, I shan't be going out anywhere, but Matthew said he might stop by after work, barring any last-minute hitches. I thought I'd put together a chicken casserole. Something that won't spoil with waiting.'

'I won't keep you, then,' he said briskly, getting to his feet and pushing papers into his briefcase. He left the room a moment later without giving her a backward glance.

Jessica felt strangely drained of emotion after he'd gone. It was an odd sensation, this blank emptiness within her, and, try as she might, she couldn't shake it off.

She left for home within the half-hour, stopping off at the shops to pick up a few groceries on the way, and then dropping by her mother's house. She liked to call in on her parents before going back to the flat. They usually chatted for half an hour or so about this and that, and then she would make her way home, replete with tea and scones.

Jonathan Reid was a retired teacher, but he still liked to put in the odd few days in school, here and there. He was always home about this time of the day, though, and she could rely on him to have the kettle on the boil. Her mother, more often than not, would appear from her workroom when she heard Jessica arrive, hair awry and hands covered with clay from the pot she had been working on. She had a small kiln, and some of her designs were on sale in the local shops. The small coffee-table in Jessica's flat was topped with tiles made by her mother.

Jessica didn't feel much like eating this afternoon, and her scone finished up more crumbled on her plate than anywhere else.

'Are you all right?' her mother asked. 'You look a bit pale.'

'I'm fine, Mum,' she said, injecting a note of cheerfulness into her voice. 'Too much to eat at lunchtime.'

It was a white lie, but her mother seemed to accept it, and the talk turned to other things, like the state of the nation, the state of the house, and her father's attempts at decorating the bathroom.

After a while Jessica stood up to go, and her father came with her to the door to see her off.

'It hasn't been getting any easier for you, has it?' he probed quietly. 'Are you sure you did the right thing when you called off the wedding?'

She thought about it before she answered. 'I don't think I could have done anything differently,' she said carefully. 'You said yourself that you waited five years for Suzy to come along, and you were beginning to despair of ever having children. Then it was another nine years before I appeared on the scene. Perhaps it would be different if Nick was an only child, if he wasn't so keen to have a family. But I couldn't face seeing my marriage disintegrate because his hopes were gradually fading away. I've seen him at work with the youngsters who come into the surgery. He's so good with them—it makes me. . . It just wouldn't be fair. . .'

She stiffened her shoulders and stepped out on to the drive. 'I'm doing OK. Don't worry about me, Dad. You just concentrate on getting that bathroom tiled before Mum gets her hands on it. You know what'll happen then. . .she'll start on a creative tack, and that'll mean major reconstruction.'

'Tell me about it!' he laughed. 'You take care, my girl. Chin up.'

She cycled on homewards, breathing in great gulps of air. Perhaps she ought to quit this job. Start up somewhere else. . .

She turned the thought over in her head for a while, but she knew it wasn't really the answer. She wasn't a quitter, was she? She'd always got on with things, no matter how difficult they might appear, and she'd go on doing that now, even if it did seem at times as though she was setting out on an uphill climb.

# CHAPTER SIX

APRIL slid away, and the new month opened with the welcome sight of a bright rising sun that spread its light into every corner of the centre. Jessica lifted her face to its golden glow, a smile curving her mouth. It was going to be warm later today. Even at this early hour in the cooler parts of the centre the sun streamed through the windows, so fiercely that they had to turn some of the blinds to an angle that would filter out its brilliant rays.

'Morning, Jessica,' Martyn greeted her as she checked into Reception. He'd been talking to Nick, but now he turned around to face her full on, and added, 'We're short-handed today. Beth's off sick, so I wondered if you would take over the child immunisations until further notice?'

It was the morning for the baby clinic, she recalled. Infants of two, three and four months would be brought in for their three-in-one and polio vaccine. She made a conscious effort to stop the edges of her smile from wavering.

'Of course. What's wrong with Beth?'

'A broken leg, I'm afraid. Apparently she fell down some steps in the garden—it was getting dark and some garden tools had been left out. Anyway, she'll be laid up for some time by all accounts, and we need to make arrangements to cover for her. I'd rather you take over the clinic, and we'll rearrange part of your schedule to suit.'

'I'll go and get organised.' She nodded briefly to Nick and walked quickly out of Reception before anything in her expression could give her away.

Had Nick had something to do with the new arrangement? It wouldn't surprise her. He seemed intent one way or another on getting her to work with children the way she had used to.

Setting out extra chairs in the large empty waiting-room, she thought of all the mothers who would be trooping in some time in the next hour with their babes in arms, and winced. It had to happen sooner or later, she told herself. There had to come a point where she was asked to take on something like this, and she couldn't go on forever fighting to avoid it, or people would start to ask questions. Questions she didn't want to answer.

'Is something wrong?'

She looked up with a start to see Nick standing in front of her. There was a serious slant to his mouth as his glance flicked over her, dark and searching.

'Wrong?' she echoed. 'Of course nothing's wrong. Why should you think that?'

'You were looking pretty grim-faced just now. Is there a problem?'

'Only in your imagination,' she retorted. 'I'm busy, that's all. I was expecting to be doing a hypertension clinic this morning, and now I'm with mums and babes, so I need to get my act in order. If I looked grim, you must have misinterpreted my expression.'

His eyes narrowed. 'Don't think I'm fooled,

Jessica,' he said crisply. 'Not by you, not for a minute. You forget, I know you too well.'

'Not well enough, apparently.' She finished a row of chairs and eyed them critically, doing a swift count in her head. These clinics always took over part of the main waiting-room. The smaller one was totally inadequate for the numbers. 'I've told you, everything's fine. I have work to do, things to organise.'

'*Something's* wrong,' he said again. 'I wasn't sure to begin with, I thought it was down to the fact that you and I had something going, one time, and that was making you tense, but it's more than that. I want to know, Jessica. Whatever it is.'

'There is nothing at all the matter with me,' she repeated firmly. 'Shouldn't you be getting ready for surgery? Going through the post? Signing repeat prescriptions? I thought there were always a thousand and one things that had to be done in a morning.'

She turned away from him and walked into the treatment-room, but he wasn't being shaken off so easily. He was like a dog with a bone between his teeth and he had no intention of giving it up.

'It isn't like you to pull back from doing things. You were always flexible, easygoing. What's the matter with you?'

'I wasn't aware that I'd refused to do anything,' she returned coolly. 'I've done whatever's required of me, and I think I've done it well, to the best of my ability. But if you mean that I was reluctant to take on the asthma clinic, then yes, that's true. I had reservations about it, and I believed they were well founded. There's no rule that says I'm not allowed to express my doubts, is there?'

'The clinic was just the start of it. I get the feeling that you're reining yourself in all the time, and that isn't like you. I want to know why you're doing it, I want to know what the hell's going on.'

'Nothing's going on. I'm busy, and you're in my way, Nick.' She stepped back and waited for him to move, but he stood his ground.

'It's the children, isn't it? You really *don't* want to work with children any more. Why?'

A prickling sensation began to work its way along her spine. He wasn't going to let up at all, was he? She didn't know how she was going to deal with this. She wasn't prepared. . . Already her heart was beginning to race uncomfortably, pumping at twice its normal speed so that she could feel it pounding against her ribcage.

'I don't have to explain my actions to you,' she said through her teeth. 'I've told you, your imagination's working overtime, and if you don't want to accept that then that's fine by me. But I have to get on, and you're stopping me from doing my job. Please get out of the way.'

'You were always good with children. . .babies especially,' he persisted. 'It was your vocation. Sometimes I used to think you made them get better through sheer force of will. Time and time again, you stayed over your shift to see that they were on the mend. You loved those babies, they were your life.' He stared at her, his mouth a taut, harsh line. 'Before we split you were going to start work on neonatal. You were excited about it, you couldn't wait to get started. What happened, Jessica? What went wrong?'

He had struck a nerve with his talk of neonatal, and it took all she had not to flinch. It had been too much, working with those tiny, helpless infants. It had been the final straw, the thing that had broken her up and cracked the emotional floodgates wide open.

She'd left the job, been off sick for two months, and they'd put it down to nervous exhaustion. Well, maybe that was right. She still felt exhausted. She couldn't take much more.

'Will you stop this?' she said tersely. 'So I enjoyed my work. I did it for a few years and then I wanted a change, I wanted to try something different. That's no crime, but to hear you talk you'd think it was. Get off my back, Nick. I've had enough of being quizzed.'

'Did something happen? Something you couldn't take?' He moved towards her, his strong hands circling her arms so that there was no way of escape. His dark eyes searched her face. 'It did, didn't it? Something happened to turn you away from it.' He made a grimace. 'Maybe I can guess. We're in a tough profession, Jessica. Sometimes things happen that are out of our control, and we end up feeling so completely helpless. There's nothing to be done about that. It's bad enough when we're dealing with adults, but when something bad happens to a child, when a child dies, a part of you goes too. It happens all the time. In the end we just have to accept it, come to terms with it. You grieve for the child, and you grieve with the parents, but you can't keep looking back. It would cripple you. You have to go on, look straight ahead and do what you can for the others. There's no other way. You know that, don't you?'

'I know that,' she said, her voice breaking, her mouth beginning to tremble. 'Nick, for God's sake, let me go. I can't handle this, I can't——'

He pulled her to him then, and she tried to push him away, hitting out at his chest with the flat of her hands, but he wasn't having any of it. He drew her into his arms, and it was too much; all at once the fight went out of her. She buried her face in his shirt front, her chest heaving as she gulped back the sobs that were trapped inside her, and his hand came up to stroke her hair, his arm holding her safe against the refuge of his body.

'Cry it out,' he said softly, his voice soothing, melting over her like warm honey. 'Let it go, Jessica. It's time to let it go.'

She did cry then, the banked tears spilling over and trickling slowly down her cheeks. She cried quietly into his shirt, grieving for the child she might never have, grieving for all the love she had inside her for this man, who could never be hers, simply because she loved him too much.

She stayed locked in his arms for a long time, until all her tears were spent, and her shaking had subsided, and then she fidgeted a little and whispered raggedly, 'I'm all right now. I don't know what came over me. I'm OK, I'll be fine. Really I will. I'm sorry about that.'

Gently he placed a finger under her chin and tilted her head back so that he could look properly into her eyes. 'Are you sure you're all right?'

She nodded, getting herself slowly back together again, and she would have moved back, away from him, except that he made no effort to let her go, but kept her close, keeping her in the circle of his arms.

'Do you want me to tell Martyn there's been a change of plan? That you're not feeling well?'

'No. I can cope now. It was silly of me, breaking down like that. I should never have let it happen; I should be more in control.'

'We're not robots, Jess. We're just ordinary, fallible human beings trying to make sense of the world we live in. Don't push yourself so hard.' Idly he smoothed the damp tendrils of hair back from her cheek, tucking the silky strands behind her ear. 'Are you sure you can manage?'

'Certain,' she said. She didn't look at him when she said that, but stared down at his chest instead, and was horrified to focus on a wet patch on the fine cotton where she'd rested her head. 'I've made an awful mess of your shirt,' she said in sudden agitation. 'Let me find a tissue or something.'

'Don't worry about it,' he murmured, smiling faintly. 'If anyone asks I'll say I spilled coffee down myself and did a repair job in the washroom.'

She tried an answering smile. 'Perhaps I'd better go and splash my face,' she said, 'and see if I can repair some of the damage. I must look awful.'

She twisted in his arms, and he slowly released her. 'If you want to talk, any time,' he suggested quietly, 'I'm always around. It might help, you know. Anything's better than bottling it up inside you.'

'Thanks,' she said, and tried to sound as though she meant it, but she knew it was one offer she wouldn't be taking up. He was the last person in the world she could confide in.

'Chin up,' he told her as he walked away, and just then he sounded so much like her father that she could have wept all over again.

That wouldn't do, of course. She'd been enough of a water spout already, and it was time she sorted herself out and got on with things. Not just with the clinic. With her life. Because Nick was right. You couldn't keep looking back, you had to go on, get on with the way things were, deal with what was happening now. She'd do that from now on, or at least she'd have a damn good try.

By the time the mothers began to arrive at the centre with their offspring, she had herself back under control, and managed to greet them with a cheerful smile.

'I can't bear to watch,' one young mum told her, cuddling her infant child before she gently removed his outer garments. 'I hate the thought of him having a needle stuck in him.'

'So do I,' Jessica murmured. 'I just feel I want to get the whole thing over and done with. He's gorgeous, isn't he?' She placed a finger gently on the baby's palm, and he made a little fist, clutching hard. 'You're lovely,' she told him. 'I'm sorry about this, but it won't take above a second or two.'

When the deed was done he gave an outraged

cry, and his mother rocked him to and fro in her arms until he forgot about what had happened to him.

'Now for the polio one,' Jessica said. 'Open your mouth, poppet. That's the way. Good boy. We're all done now.' She turned her attention back to the mother. 'Do you know about the need for taking care over his nappy changes for the next week or so? Don't let anyone who hasn't been vaccinated have anything to do with them without taking great care. There is a slight risk of infection.'

'I heard about that,' the girl said, dressing the child once more while Jessica filled in the details on the immunisation card. 'I'm pretty sure my husband was vaccinated as a child, but I'll check.'

The next mother came in looking anxious. 'I know her appointment's for today, but I don't know whether she ought to have the jab,' she said. 'She's been really fretful just lately, and I don't know whether she's coming down with something.'

'She does look a bit hot,' Jessica agreed, running the back of her hand lightly over the child's forehead. 'And her breathing does sound quite chesty. Perhaps you should let one of the doctors have a look at her. We don't have to give her the injection today; you can bring her in again whenever she's back on form. It's best to leave it a while if she's off colour. Have a word with the receptionist, and she'll perhaps be able to fit you in with one of the doctors this morning.'

'Shall I need to make another appointment with you?'

'No, just bring her along to the clinic. There'll be no problem.'

The queue outside the treatment-room gradually dwindled, and Jessica sighed with relief when the last tiny patient had been taken away. It hadn't been nearly as bad as she'd thought. She'd been far too busy to let her emotions get in the way of what she was doing, though there was no denying she'd have loved to hold one or two of those soft little bundles and croon them to sleep in her arms. The quiet, peaceful ones, anyway. Some of them had been making enough noise to shatter glass, and for her ears' sake she was definitely thankful they were going home with someone else!

She began to stack the chairs that wouldn't be needed any more, and a man sidestepped to avoid getting in her way. She glanced up at him.

'Mr Templeton,' she said. 'How are you? Have you been to the hospital yet?'

He smiled at her and nodded. 'I went about three weeks ago. It wasn't so bad. Like you said, they gave me something so I wasn't too bothered about having it done. I'd have liked to watch it on screen though. It isn't every day you get the chance to see your innards, but the monitor was to the back of me, and they wouldn't let me face that way.' He shrugged and grinned crookedly. 'I've just been in to see Dr Castlemaine to get the results. It takes a while, doesn't it, for all the paperwork to get from there to here? Anyway, everything's fine. It's all clear, nothing nasty, just some ulceration, and the doc's given me some tablets to sort that out.'

'I'm glad about that. I told you you were working too hard, didn't I? Is there any way you can ease up a bit?'

'That's just what the doc said. A change of lifestyle's what's needed, but that's easier said than done, isn't it?'

'That's true enough. But it might be worth sitting down and seeing if there are some things you can deal with differently.'

She didn't know why she was giving him advice like that. Who was she to comment on lifestyle? She'd changed hers, and she wasn't sure now whether it was for the better, the way things were turning out. Still, she wasn't going to dwell on that. The future was what mattered, and she was going to concentrate on making it a good one.

She walked over to Reception, waving a casual hand as Richard Templeton went out through the main door. She could do with a coffee, and company, right now.

The midwife and local health visitor must have had the same idea.

'Another name for Sarah's list,' the midwife was saying. 'He's a beautiful little boy. Looks just like his father.'

The health visitor laughed. 'Honestly, Jane, I don't know how you can say that, when he's just a few days old. I can hardly ever see any likenesses, even when they're pointed out to me.'

'Who are we talking about?' Jessica wanted to know.

'Catherine Markham's little boy,' Jane told her. 'He was born just a few days ago. I've been round to the house this morning, and he's doing fine.

They've called him Rhys. It's an unusual name, isn't it? I like it.'

Jessica nodded. 'How is Catherine? Sarah was keeping a check on her sugar levels all the way through, wasn't she? To begin with we thought the baby might be on the large side.'

'No, everything was fine, he weighed in at seven and a half pounds—twenty-three inches long. He's going to be tall, I'll bet, like his dad.'

'I think you've a soft spot for his dad,' Helen put in with a chuckle, and Jessica smiled and went to pour herself a drink.

She was on duty on Saturday morning the following week. It was usually a light surgery, since they only saw emergencies, things that had cropped up suddenly and couldn't be left till Monday. They worked a rota system, so she only worked one in four, and she didn't mind that at all. It was just a couple of hours, and it gave her the chance to catch up on her paperwork if they weren't busy.

It was hot today and she hadn't planned on doing anything more energetic than cycling to and from the centre. Except she'd bargained without the punctured tyre, and now it looked as though she was going to have to walk home, wheeling the wretched thing for a couple of miles. It served her right, really. She'd known the repair outfit needed replacing last week, and she'd done nothing about it.

'I could give you a lift,' Nick said. 'We could put the bike in the back of my car. There's plenty of room. It depends how much of a hurry you're in. Only I have to stop by Gemma Cresswell's house and pay her a visit.'

Jessica frowned. 'The little girl who had the renal problems? She went into failure, didn't she?'

'That's right. She's on dialysis now, CAPD, and I want to check that she's coping. There was a problem with peritonitis, and now her mother thinks she's very depressed.'

'That's not surprising, is it, in the circumstances? What's happened to her must take some getting used to, though at least CAPD will give her more freedom to get about.'

Continuous ambulatory peritoneal dialysis was far less restrictive than other forms of dialysis. Gemma wouldn't have to sit for hours connected to a machine, and by now she'd probably learned to cope efficiently with the relatively simple procedures of changing the bags of fluid.

'I'd like to come with you,' she said. 'And I'd be glad of a lift, if it's no trouble. I wasn't looking forward to a long walk home. It's such a beautiful day, I don't want to do much of anything. I don't think I can even be bothered to cook lunch. Perhaps I'll just make do with a sandwich and get the lounger out.'

'I feel the same way,' he said, taking in a leisurely breath and flexing his shoulder muscles. 'We could always stop by the pub afterwards and grab a bite to eat. They do good meals at the Waterside. What do you think?'

He made the suggestion casually, and she could hardly come up with an excuse now. He already knew she wasn't planning on having visitors this afternoon.

'It sounds like a great idea,' she agreed. 'But I can hardly go anywhere dressed like this.'

His glance skimmed over her blue uniform. 'That's OK. We'll drop the bike off first, and you can slip into something cool.'

There was no way of backing out, and if she was honest with herself she didn't really want to try. The thought of spending a few snatched hours with him was irresistible. Perhaps she was being foolhardy, living dangerously, but if she took great care, if she steeled herself to keep the barriers in place, there was no reason she would come to regret it, was there?

# CHAPTER SEVEN

GEMMA CRESSWELL lived in one of the newer detached houses on a nearby estate. Her mother answered the door to Nick and Jessica, and said with a slightly worried edge to her voice, 'She's in her room, listening to tapes. Go through to the lounge, won't you, and I'll see if I can persuade her to come downstairs? I'll just be a minute or two.'

'If she's reluctant to come down,' Nick suggested quickly, 'perhaps it would be better if we went up to her. She might feel more comfortable on her own territory.'

'Oh.' Mrs Cresswell was taken aback for a moment, but then said, 'Well, all right, if you think it's best. Her room's usually in a terrible state, though. I hope you won't mind. She's so untidy.'

'We shan't mind at all,' he said with a smile. 'But before we go up, perhaps I could take a look at the effluent you saved to show me.'

'Of course.'

She went and fetched it, and Nick held the bag of yellow fluid up to the light and said with satisfaction, 'That looks fine. No worries on that score.'

He put it to one side, and they followed as Mrs Cresswell led the way upstairs. She tapped lightly on her daughter's door before pushing it open.

'The doctor's here to see you, Gemma, and he's brought a nurse along with him. Good heavens,' she said with a gasp as she looked around, 'what a mess it is in here.' She began hastily to pick up things from the floor and tidy up books that lay scattered on shelves against one wall. 'It's even worse than I thought.'

Jessica grinned. 'Oh, I don't know about that. My room used to look much the same. In fact, it still does sometimes. I maintain it has a lived-in look.' She went over to the young girl, who was sitting on the bed, and said cheerfully, 'Hello, Gemma. I'm Jessica Reid. I hope you don't mind my coming along with Dr Tyler to see you. He's giving me a lift home because my bike threw a puncture. He's told me all about you, and I was glad when he said I could come along. I've been wanting to meet you.'

Gemma shrugged. 'I don't mind.' She looked small and thin, her face pinched and pale-looking against a straight fall of black hair.

'How are you feeling, Gemma?' Nick asked, sitting down beside the girl.

The thin shoulders lifted again. 'I'm all right, I guess.'

'And are you coping with the bags? Any problems?'

'It's OK, I suppose. Mum helps me sometimes. But I can do it for myself.'

'That's very good; I'm glad to hear it. I'd like to check your temperature,' he murmured, reaching for his thermometer and sliding it under her tongue. 'I think you're managing very well, Gemma, and your effluent looks just as it should.'

He removed the thermometer after a moment or two, glancing at it before replacing it in its container. 'That's good, too. I think I should just quickly check your tummy while I'm here. Could you lie back on the bed for a minute or two?'

He gently examined the site of the catheter, checking the connector and tubing, and said in a while, 'That looks fine, sweetheart. You can cover up now.'

Jessica helped the little girl with her clothes and then, while Nick was busy checking the child's blood pressure, asked, 'Do you go back to the hospital for check-ups every so often?'

Gemma nodded, and said dully, 'About once a month.'

'I expect you've missed quite a lot of school this term, haven't you, one way and another? Do you miss your friends? Or have they been coming to visit?'

'Sometimes they come. But I'll be going back next week, anyway.'

'Are you looking forward to that?'

Another shrug. 'I suppose so.'

Nick talked quietly to the girl's mother, and Jessica glanced around the room and let her gaze settle on the cassette tapes which were lying in an untidy heap on the dressing table. She picked up an empty case and inspected the label.

'Is this what you were listening to before we came?' She recognised the name of the band. 'They're top of the charts just now, aren't they? I went to a concert of theirs a couple of years ago. I thought they were great fun.'

Gemma brightened a fraction, enough to show

Jessica the rest of her collection, but before they could get too engrossed Nick was signalling that it was time to leave.

In his car a few minutes later, Jessica said quietly, 'I think her mother's right. She's definitely depressed. But, once she gets back to school and mixes with her friends, things might improve.'

'We'll keep our fingers crossed,' Nick said, taking off his jacket and throwing it on the back seat. His tie followed, and he slid a finger inside his collar, releasing the top couple of buttons. 'Hot in here, isn't it? This heat's been building up all morning.' He turned his key in the ignition and the engine growled into life. 'Children are normally tremendously resilient, and physically she's doing fine, but this whole thing has come as an enormous shock to her and to the family. It'll probably take a while longer before she comes to terms with what's happened to her.'

He wound down the window to let some cool air circulate, then set the car in motion, driving smoothly along the country roads. It didn't take long before they reached the next village, and found the turn-off for Jessica's flat.

'Is this it?' he asked, approaching the grocery store, and she nodded.

'You should be able to park around the back. We have our own little corner of the car park, and I usually lock my bike away there. There are two flats, and there's a private entrance to each, tucked away at the side.'

He swung the car into the parking slot, and switched off the engine. Getting out from behind the wheel, he pushed the door shut and stared up at the building, shielding his eyes against the sun.

'I have to say it, Jess,' he said, frowning, 'this is not you. Definitely not you.'

'I'll stow the bike away,' she murmured, steadfastly refusing to let his comments get to her, and searching in her bag for the door key. She passed it across to him. 'Let yourself into the flat, will you? It's the one with the blue door.'

'I don't suppose they sell puncture kits in the store?' he asked, ignoring the key and going around to the back of the car to lift out the bike.

She shook her head. 'I'll have to pay a visit to the bike shop on Main Street later on this afternoon.'

'I'll do it for you now. It won't take me above a few minutes to go and pick one up. Then when I get back I'll fix the tyre.'

She was touched by his offer. 'That's very thoughtful of you.' There wasn't really any reason why his offer should surprise her. He had always been considerate and caring, and just thinking about the kind of man he was brought a lump to her throat. 'But you don't need to, you know. I can do it later.'

'It's no trouble. I'll see to it while you get changed.'

'Thanks.' She smiled at him. 'Would you like a cold drink to keep you going? I think there's some lager in the fridge.'

'Sounds like a good idea,' he said. 'This heat's making me parched. But I'll have it when I get back.'

'OK. Come up when you're ready. I'll leave it

out for you in the kitchen. That's on the right, just past the bathroom.'

She ran up the metal stairs that flanked the side of the building, and let herself into the flat. Before she did anything else she poured herself a cooling fruit juice and swallowed it down, enjoying the way it eased her dry throat. Then she placed a can of cold lager and a glass on the kitchen table for Nick.

Sitting in the car had made her feel hot and sticky, and the thought of a quick shower was getting more and more tempting by the minute. Nick would probably be busy for a while, so she might as well grab the chance.

She fetched a handful of clean underwear from the bedroom, and spent some time searching through her wardrobe looking for something to wear. Something light and simple. Her fingers came to rest on a dress of delicately patterned cotton in summery hues of rose-pink and palest green tints. It was her favourite, but. . .she hesitated. . .she wanted to look good, but she didn't want him to think she'd dressed up specially for him. Though, if she was honest with herself, that was exactly what she did want to do. She wanted to look good in his eyes, she wanted him to be pleased with what he saw when he looked at her.

She stifled a moan. What was she thinking of? This was going nowhere; she must be crazy to even contemplate spending time with him. She should call it off, put an end to this madness right now. . .

Some demon inside her had taken over. There

was no other answer as to why she found herself reaching for the dress and hurrying with it into the bathroom.

The water washed over her skin in a cooling stream, and she stood under the spray just long enough to let it rinse away the slick of perfumed soap and leave her feeling refreshed. She'd have liked to stay a few minutes more, just quietly relaxing, but she didn't want to keep Nick waiting. As it was, she'd taken longer than she'd intended.

Hastily she dried herself on a soft towel, then slipped into lacy bra and briefs before reaching for the dress and tugging it off its hanger.

The door opened just then, and Nick walked in. She stared at him, her mind moving dazedly like a film rolling in slow motion as she took in the sight of him standing there in her bathroom. The sleeves of his shirt were pushed back to reveal strong, sun-browned forearms covered with a smattering of dark hair. His hands were wet, she realised, blinking; droplets of water were falling to the floor, one or two trickling slowly backwards along his arms.

He had come to a sudden halt, the door falling shut behind him. He made no attempt to move, but stared in return, his expression arrested, as though he, too, was caught up in that same slow-moving reel.

After a moment or two he shook his head, as if that might clear it, then he said softly, 'I'm sorry. I came looking for a towel. I assumed you would be in the bedroom.' His gaze moved over her, gliding over the soft swell of her breast and slowly shifting to rest on the shapely curve of her hips.

'I should have been.' Her voice sounded odd, a little shaky, and she tried again. 'I thought I'd have time for a quick shower. I didn't mean to take so long.'

'I think I'm glad you did. You're beautiful, Jessica. Exquisite. . .' His glance moved hotly to her face. 'I'd almost forgotten. . .'

Her breathing quickened, her breasts rising and falling in fast tempo as she struggled for air. Her pulse was racing, pounding a staccato rhythm so fierce that she could feel it hammering in her throat, filling her ears with the roar of blood.

He was very still, waiting, his spine stiffened, as though every sense he possessed was heightened, alerted for action. He was just a heartbeat away. She swayed a little. All she had to do was move a step closer, and he would fold her into his arms. . .

'Nick. . .I. . .we. . .'

She couldn't let this happen. It was tearing her apart, but there was no future for them together, she'd known it before and she knew it now, and it was a silent scream running through her head.

Her fingers closed in a tight spasm on the fabric of the dress. 'I must get dressed,' she muttered hoarsely, not looking at him. 'This isn't going to work, is it? There are too many memories, too many things to get in the way. Perhaps we should forget all about lunch. Maybe you should go.'

'And maybe we should get on with life and forget all about the past. We have to work together, to see each other every day and mix with other staff at the centre as though we're nothing more than colleagues. How can we do that, if every time we're together we're on edge?' His sharp tone brought her gaze winging upwards. 'I think we should have lunch, just as we planned. I'll wait for you in the sitting-room. But get a move-on. They get pretty busy later on.'

He walked out and left her to it, and she took a few gulping breaths to steady herself. It was probably true, what he had said. If they left things as they were they'd be twitching every time they came near one another at work, and that just wouldn't do at all. They had to learn to relax in each other's company, Nick was right about that, and he was prepared to make an effort to that end. It was up to her to calm down and meet him halfway.

The Waterside pub was already crowded with people when they arrived there about twenty minutes later. There was hardly room to move in the narrow bar, and every table in the restaurant area was taken. Outside, though, on the wide grassed area by the sweeping expanse of water, there were one or two bench tables that were still unoccupied. Jessica commandeered one, while Nick went to place their order.

She sat and watched the swans glide by, dipping their graceful necks every now and then for a tasty titbit thrown by children who walked up to the water's edge. There were ducks as well, paddling closer so as not to miss out. Jessica smiled as she watched them.

'It's pleasant here, isn't it?' Nick remarked, setting drinks down on the table, and sliding into the seat opposite. 'I always feel I can unwind here, and watch the world go by, just for a while. Are you sure you don't mind eating outside?'

'I think I prefer it. At least we're not in the full sun here, with the shrubbery at the back and those trees giving a bit of shade. I'm not complaining about the heat, mind. This freak weather's a bonus, like summer come early.'

Their meals arrived, and Jessica inspected her salad with satisfaction. 'I hadn't realised quite how hungry I was,' she said, spearing a succulent morsel of red capsicum.

They ate in silence for a while, then turned to watch as a canal boat manoeuvred alongside the canal bank, waiting for the lock further on to fill up.

'I quite like the idea of boating,' she murmured. 'Just spending a quiet afternoon on the river. I don't know about canals, though. I'm not sure I've the patience to cope with all those lock gates.'

'Oh, I don't know,' Nick commented mildly. 'It's all part of the fun, the men doing the difficult job of steering, the womenfolk operating the gates.'

'That's a very sexist remark,' she said grittily, and he laughed.

'Maybe. We could always try it one day, and you could show off your navigation skills.'

'Since I doubt you've ever been at the helm of anything larger than a paddle boat, they're probably every bit as good as yours,' she retorted, but the sting in her tone was muted, since her mind was taken up with visions of the two of them on board a sleek canal boat; she would be at the wheel, and Nick would have his arms very firmly around her. She could almost feel the touch of his warm lips on her cheek. . .

A commotion started up near-by, and she jerked her gaze to where the noise was coming from. A woman was making a keening sound, and at first Jessica thought she was hurt; then when she saw that she wasn't, she wondered if someone might have fallen in the water. A child, perhaps. She got to her feet at the same time as Nick, and sent a swift glance to the water, but there wasn't more than a gentle ripple on its surface.

'It must be the baby,' Nick said, moving towards the man and woman who had been sitting some distance from them, on the grass. Jessica had noticed the child. About ten or so months old, she had thought, perhaps a year. Now she could see that the woman was holding the baby in her arms, rocking it against her chest, her face crumpled with distress. She hurried after Nick.

'Is something the matter?' he was saying. 'I'm a doctor. . .can I do anything to help?'

'Oh, thank God,' the woman said urgently. 'Her eyes are rolling. . .I don't know what to do. She's not responding to me, she's not with me at all.'

'Shall I take her?' Nick said. 'Let's see if we can get her inside, somewhere cool.'

Jessica went ahead of him and spoke quickly to the landlord, explaining what had happened. 'Do you have a quiet room?' she asked. 'Somewhere we can take the child?'

He nodded and lifted up the bar hatch. 'Bring her through here,' he said, and Nick went into the small sitting-room beyond, followed by the worried parents.

'Is there anything I can do?' the landlord asked.

'We'll need water,' Jessica told him. 'Tepid. And a flannel or sponge, if you have one.'

He nodded. 'Will do.'

'I think she's had a touch too much sun,' Nick was telling the parents. The child was lying across his knees, and Jessica could see that her eyes had turned upwards and her little face was very flushed. 'What we need to do is reduce her temperature very quickly, so I'm going to take off some of her things and let the air get to her. Then we'll sponge her down with cool water.' He was busy all the time he was speaking, and by the time the landlord returned with a bowl and sponge the child was freed of her vest and Jessica was fanning her lightly with a thin book she had discovered on the coffee-table.

Nick gently bathed the baby's face with the sponge that had been dipped in cool water, while Jessica found a flannel and worked on her chest and tummy.

'I think she's beginning to come out of it,' Nick said quietly, continuing with the water treatment. 'Her eyes are coming back to normal.'

The girl's father hovered near by. 'Hannah, sweetheart, it's Daddy,' he said now. 'Look at me, baby, can you see me? Here's Mummy as well. Can you see Mummy?'

'I think she can,' Jessica murmured. 'She's

beginning to focus. Just give her a minute or two to adjust.'

'Panic over,' Nick said a while later, handing the child back to her mother. 'I think she'll be all right now. Give her a cool drink, if you can, to replace any fluid she's lost, and if you have any more worries about her, call your local doctor or take her along to Casualty. But I'm pretty sure she'll be all right as long as you keep her cool.'

'Too much exposure to heat's never a good idea,' Jessica added. 'It might be helpful to get her to wear a sun hat if ever she's going to be exposed to the sun.'

'We'll do that,' the young mother said vehemently. 'I've never been so frightened in my life. It happened so suddenly—it was such a shock.'

'We can never thank you enough,' Hannah's father said, looking at Nick. 'I didn't know what was happening, but you were marvellous.'

'It's OK,' Nick murmured. 'We were glad to help.'

He stood the landlord a drink, then took Jessica's arm and led her outside.

'Shall we take a walk along the canal path? I fancy watching the water for a while, but I'd sooner do it in peace and quiet.'

She nodded. 'That sounds like a good idea.'

They walked along for a while, making desultory conversation as they left the pub behind and followed the water course through the nearby field. A brightly painted canal boat passed them by, and a dog on deck leaped about excitedly, wagging its tail and making them laugh at its comical antics.

'It's amazing that he doesn't fall in, careering about like that,' Nick said. 'But I expect he's a seasoned sailor by now.'

'Looks that way.'

They walked on until they came to a smooth patch of grass, and Nick suggested that they sit down for a while.

'I felt sorry for that baby's parents,' he said quietly. 'They looked so young, little more than kids themselves.'

'It's frightening to see something like that,' Jessica agreed. 'I remember when I was a teenager my cousin's baby suffered from convulsions. It scared me at first, but then I wanted to do something about it. I think that's what started me off thinking seriously about becoming a nurse. My parents thought it was a good idea. They said they'd known it was the only career for me when I started practising on the family pets.'

'The pets?' He looked at her quizzically, and she explained.

She curled her arms comfortably around her bent knees. 'I was getting a little tired of bandaging my dolls and teddies, you know, and they could never take the medicine properly, without getting into a sticky mess. So I started binding up the rabbit's legs, and putting sticking plaster on the guinea pigs till my mum and dad suggested it wasn't such a good idea. They were glad of my help with the dog, though.'

'You bandaged the dog?'

'No, no, she'd never sit still long enough for

that. The thing with her was, she'd never take the tablets the vet prescribed. She was terrible about them. She absolutely hated taking them, and she'd give you a real runaround until you finally caught her and dropped one down her throat and clamped her jaws shut. Then, just when you finally got to thinking you'd won and she'd swallowed them, she'd disappear into a corner and spit them out. You couldn't even crush them up in a drink, as she'd realise what you were up to.'

He chuckled. 'She was definitely a problem patient.'

'Oh, I sorted her out in the end. What you had to do was buy her some soft-centred chocolates. Then you'd slip a tablet into the middle of one and she'd scoff it down faster than you could say "cats". It was easy after that. She could never get enough of strawberry creams.'

He laughed at that. 'Did you never think of being a vet?'

'Not really. I gave it some passing thought, but I didn't think I'd be very good at handling some of the larger animals, or dealing with the ones that wanted to bite me. Human patients are much more docile and easy to manage.'

'Most, perhaps. At least you can communicate with them more easily.' His amused glance travelled slowly over her face, then he sobered a little, and she suddenly realised how very close together they were sitting, almost touching. He said softly, 'We knew each other so well, you and I. I thought I knew everything about you. Your childhood, your family, your dreams. We shared such a lot.'

Remembering, she turned her gaze blindly out over the water.

'That was a long time ago,' she said in a choked voice.

'Yes.'

He reached out to her then, trailing one long finger along the hairline of her brow and down over her temple, and she felt the sensation quiver right down her body to the very tips of her toes. His hand cupped her face, turning her towards him, and she knew that he was going to kiss her. As he bent his head nearer she lifted her face to his and closed her eyes, blotting out the sun, pushing everything from her mind except for this wonderful moment.

His mouth touched hers, a drifting, feather-like brush of his lips over hers, and the world spiralled off course with dizzying speed. She was out of synch with everything, thrown off balance, and none of it mattered, the only thing she cared about was being here with him, wrapped securely in his arms as though he would never let her go.

He crushed her to him, deepening the kiss, and tipping her back into the cushioning, sweet-scented grass. His arm supported her shoulders, his free hand lifted to caress the soft fullness of her breast, and she moved into the warmth of his body, murmurs of longing muffled against his mouth, her body pliant with desire. She wanted him so much, it was like a fever growing in her, burning her up.

She felt the fever in him, too, the urgency of a desire equal to her own. His breathing was fast, his heart thudding an erratic tattoo against his ribcage. She heard him whisper her name, a hoarse, ragged sound, and she opened her eyes to gaze into the flickering depths of his.

Her fingers curled into the muscled hardness of his chest, aching to feel the velvet smoothness beneath his shirt. She slid her hand upwards, delighting in the feel of him, curving her palm over the strong bones of his shoulder.

'I thought I knew everything about you,' he muttered thickly. 'Everything there was to know. But I was wrong, wasn't I? I knew about Matthew, I saw you with him nearly every day and I wanted to believe you were just friends, but I was fooling myself. God, what a fool I was.'

She drew in a shocked breath and he stared down at her. 'Don't try to deny it,' he said. 'It's too late for that.' His mouth made a taut, harsh line. 'But I do know something else, Jessica. You want me. Whatever it is you feel for Matthew, you still want me, I'm certain of that. I think you'd have gone on making love with me, in this field, in broad daylight.'

He raised his head from her and gazed into the distance. 'Another time, perhaps,' he said, and there was no mistaking the thread of bitterness that laced his tone. 'It looks as if soon we might have company, and that wouldn't do at all, would it?'

She turned to follow his glance, and saw another couple, out for an afternoon walk with their dog.

He went on coldly, 'I expect you'd pull up short at the prospect of having an audience. Even you must have some scruples.'

# CHAPTER EIGHT

IT HAD been a bad mistake, letting her guard down with Nick, but it wasn't a mistake she was likely to repeat. Jessica pulled open the drawer of the filing cabinet and flicked through the folders in there. He had taught her a sharp lesson, and she had learned it well. She wasn't going to forget in a hurry what he really thought of her.

She could hardly blame him for being bitter. However wrong he was in his assumptions, he did feel that he had been treated badly by both her and Matthew, but there was nothing she could do to change that, not without revealing the truth, and that was something she couldn't contemplate.

But, whatever he believed, it didn't give him the right to treat her like a whore, and she was finding it more and more difficult to be civil to him. She didn't know how to work with him without letting her feelings of hurt and anger show.

As it was, the asthma clinic was turning out to be a sore trial on her nerves this afternoon, but she was doing her very best to keep her manner cool and professional, not giving anything away.

To look at Nick, calm and composed as he dealt with each patient, you wouldn't have believed that interlude by the water had ever happened, and that incensed her even more. She bit down hard on her lower lip and almost drew blood. Damn him, damn, damn, damn him for being such an annoying, hateful, abominable man.

'The card, Jessica.' Nick's deep, cool tones cut into her thoughts like an arrow splintering wood, and her shoulders gave a little jerk as though he had struck her. 'Have you finished with it?'

'The what? Oh! The card. . .yes, of course.' She took in a deep breath and turned away from the open drawer of the filing cabinet, handing the record card to the patient. 'There you are, Mrs Turner. I'm sorry to have kept you waiting.'

'That's all right, love. There were a lot of notes to put down today, weren't there? I just wish there was a cure for this wretched illness. Still, we just have to keep going, don't we?'

She went out, and Nick said drily, 'If she got rid of the cats she might fare a lot better, but she won't hear of it. Both she and the child have a number of allergies, and the asthma just goes on giving them trouble.'

'The cats have been around almost as long as the boy,' Jessica remarked coldly, and shut the drawer with a bang. 'I expect they're part of the family by now.'

'You don't appear to be yourself today,' Nick murmured, his mouth making a cynical twist. 'Is something bothering you?'

'Nothing I'd want to share with you,' she returned with acid directness. 'Shall I bring in the next patient?'

'By all means, let's not keep anyone waiting.'

Somehow she managed to get through the afternoon. When they'd finished Martyn came in to talk to Nick, and she cleared up the room quickly and left the building before they were through.

She wasn't giving Nick the chance to get her alone and start taking pot-shots at her.

If her parents thought she was in any way edgy when she paid them a quick half-hour visit, they wisely said nothing, and she went off home to spend the evening working off her bad temper in a bout of cleaning.

It was even more difficult keeping up a front with her colleagues at the centre. Whenever Nick was around she did her best to appear polite and as normal as possible towards him, but it was a strain, there was no denying it, and she received one or two puzzled looks along the way.

It was Sarah who finally asked one day, when they were alone in the staff lounge, 'Are you OK, Jessica? You seem a little tense just lately. Is anything wrong?'

Jessica poured herself a coffee and reached into her pocket for a couple of paracetamol. 'I'm fine, really.' She wasn't going to confide in anyone about her problems with Nick, but she wouldn't be lying if she told Sarah what was adding to her black mood. 'If I seem uptight today, it's perhaps down to my usual monthly problem. It gets quite painful sometimes, and it tends to make me a bit snappy. I'm sorry about that. It'll settle down in a day or so.'

She tore open the foil on the tablets and swallowed them with her drink.

Sarah nodded in sympathy. 'It's no fun, is it? But have you had a check-up? If the pain's really bad you ought to go and see your doctor to find out if there's any underlying cause.'

'I did see him a while back, and I've had some

tests done, but there's no immediate remedy. I shouldn't have neglected my keep-fit exercises over the summer, that's all. I always feel better when I keep up my regular workouts.'

'Well, bear in mind what I said. If you're not happy, go back to him, or get a second opinion. There's no reason you should suffer, just because you're a woman.'

'Thanks, Sarah. I will keep it in mind.' She put her coffee-cup to her lips and just as she was about to take a sip she caught a movement across the room out of the corner of her eye. She turned to take a proper look, and saw Nick standing by the closed door.

Shakily she returned the cup to its saucer. Neither of them had heard him come into the room, and she wondered how long he had been standing there, and just how much he'd heard. Thank heaven she hadn't indulged herself in a real heart-to-heart with Sarah.

Even so, she wasn't sure she liked the thoughtful, frowning expression that narrowed his eyes and etched a line into the smoothness of his brow. She'd have given anything to know just what was going on in his head right now.

'Nick,' Sarah said with a smile. 'How was your weekend? Did you go to your parents' house?'

'I did. I stayed over for Claire's birthday party, along with practically the whole family.' He grinned. 'It was what you might call boisterous. The house was full to brimming, and there was hardly room to move, let alone get any peace.'

'Admit it,' Sarah demanded, 'you loved it.'

'Well, yes, I think I probably did. Young

Adam's learned to walk and he's into everything now, which was fun up to a point, but after a while my father and I retreated to the study for a quiet game of chess. It was OK till my mother discovered where we were.'

Sarah laughed. 'No time for any house hunting this weekend, then?'

He shook his head. 'Next week maybe. I've been given details of a couple of properties that may be possibilities. Any luck with letting your house?'

She nodded. 'A divorcee and her student daughter are moving in at the end of the month. It'll be let for at least six months, and then we'll see if they want to keep it on, or perhaps by then I might decide to sell.'

Jessica drained the last of her coffee and excused herself. 'I'd better head for the treatment-room,' she said.

'See you later,' Sarah acknowledged. 'I've scheduled that minor op for two o'clock. Will you be free to assist me then?'

'No problem,' Jessica agreed. 'I've made a note of it. A skin biopsy, wasn't it?'

'That's the one. Mrs Henderson. We'll get the tissue sent off to the lab and see what results they come up with. It's probably nothing serious, but there's quite a marked discoloration and I'd sooner be safe than sorry.'

One of Jessica's first patients after the break was five-year-old Serena Simpson. She was a pretty child, with long brown hair and eyes that were a delightful mixture of grey and blue.

'What a lovely name,' Jessica said, smiling at

the little girl. She turned to the mother. 'You don't hear it very often, do you?'

'I suppose not.' Mandy was clearly agitated this morning, and Jessica noticed that her movements were more stiff than usual. 'Take a seat,' she said. 'Are you struggling today?'

'I shouldn't have gone over the top with the cleaning yesterday,' Mandy told her. 'That's all it is.'

Jessica nodded. 'Serena can sit up here, on the couch. And Joseph,' she turned to the dark-haired little boy, 'Joseph looks as if he's just fine, standing by Mum. Now, what are we dealing with here, Serena? A clean dressing, is it? You look as though you've had a nasty scald on that arm.'

'We took her straight to Casualty after it happened,' Mandy said. 'A neighbour and me, that is. She drove me there. Then I brought her in to see Dr Lancaster this morning. He said it isn't a deep burn. . .but it's been so painful for her. She's had to have something to ease it. . .'

'It's a fact that superficial burns can be much more painful than deep ones,' Jessica agreed as she inspected the damage. 'It looks as though it's beginning to heal nicely. We just need to put on another dry gauze dressing.'

'It's all my fault,' Mandy said unhappily. 'I should have kept more of an eye on her, but I was just trying to grab five minutes' rest. I thought she was playing with Joseph. They had the Lego out on the kitchen table. It was only when I heard the crash——'

'We were trying to help,' Joseph put in seriously. 'Mummy was tired, and we thought we'd make her a cup of tea. It's what Daddy does.'

'That was very thoughtful of you,' Jessica told the children. 'But it is dangerous for you to use the kettle when Mummy and Daddy aren't watching you. You know that now, don't you?'

They both nodded solemnly. 'We were just trying to make Mummy feel good,' Serena said.

'I know, sweetheart.' She gave the girl a gentle hug. 'Tell you what, next time you want to do something nice for Mummy, how about getting her a mug of cold milk and some biscuits?'

'That would be lovely,' Mandy said. 'I'd like that. Ginger biscuits and chocolate fingers. Yummy.'

Joseph and Serena exchanged grins. 'Yummy,' they chorused.

Jessica watched them troop out a few minutes later, and her thoughts wandered to little Gemma Cresswell. Maybe she'd visit now and again just to see how she was doing. It would be nice to see her smile.

Jessica was setting out chairs again for the immunisation clinic some days later, when Sarah hurried through the waiting-room with Daniel in tow. She looked deathly pale and Jessica frowned as she watched her rush by.

'Sarah——'

'Look after Daniel for me, will you?' Sarah pleaded. 'I shan't be more than a minute or two.'

'Of course, don't worry. What is it, are you——?' But Sarah had vanished through the swing doors, in the direction of the washroom, and Jessica turned thoughtfully to Daniel.

'She's prob'ly being sick,' he announced sagely. 'She does that a lot these days. And she won't eat her cornflakes any more, but she still makes me eat mine.' His mouth pursed with indignation as he thought about the injustice. 'Daddy says they're good for me. He says Mummy's done all her growing and doesn't need them like me. Then Mummy said something and they both started laughing. I still don't think it's fair.'

Jessica ruffled his hair and drew him to her for a hug. 'I expect Mummy will start eating them again, before long. When she stops being sick.'

She stared at the closed door and told herself she was happy for Sarah, and she was, really. It would just take her a little while to get used to the idea, that was all.

'Problems?' Nick asked, coming into the waiting-room, and Jessica came out of her reverie and gathered her wits.

'None,' she said. 'We're just waiting for Sarah. A touch of morning sickness, I think.'

'Ah. . .' He grinned, had a short bout of make-believe fisticuffs with Daniel, then made his way towards Reception, whistling a tune softly as he went.

The clinic seemed busier than usual this morning, but it might just have been that Jessica had to steel her mind to concentrate, and the paperwork took twice as long to complete.

Her last patient was Catherine Markham's little boy, Rhys. He was two months old, and his eyes were a beautiful deep blue, his hair a soft brown.

'He's a handsome little lad, isn't he?' Jessica said when they were all finished and she had filled in the details on his card. 'And so good,' she murmured, touching his cheek lightly with her finger. 'His skin's so soft, isn't it? Just perfect. . . There's something about a baby's skin. . .'

Just then the baby smiled at her, a real, dimple-cheeked smile, not wind or a colicky grimace, but a real, perfect expression of recognition and delight. She smiled back at him, and Catherine said, 'Would you like to hold him? It'll give me a chance to take this jacket off. It was cool when I set out this morning, but I'm going to be far too hot by the time I get to the shops.'

'I'd love to,' Jessica said. Catherine placed him in her arms, and she rocked him gently, singing softly to him while his mother dealt with her coat and pushed it into her shopping bag.

'All done,' Catherine said. 'That feels much better.'

It was a wrench to give him back, but she handed him over and watched while he was tucked into his baby carrier.

'See you in a month's time,' she murmured, and watched as he went on his way.

'Finished?' Nick queried, putting in an appearance as the outer door closed on Catherine.

'Yes,' she said abruptly.

The waiting-room was empty now, and normally she would have cleared up and started straight away on updating her notes on the computer. Only today was different, she couldn't get herself to function on all cylinders, and she turned and walked out of the side-door and carried on walking until she found a quiet spot in the shrub garden at the back of the centre.

She found a bench seat and sat down on it, staring straight ahead at the cherry tree.

She was going to have to get to grips with this, sooner or later. There was no way she could avoid contact with children for evermore, and she couldn't contemplate a life of constant stress, fighting with her inner self. It was too hard to bear; it left her feeling drained.

Perhaps she ought never to have given up her work with sick children. Perhaps being with them was the only way she would ever come to terms with her own sense of loss.

'Feeling broody?' Nick had come up on her out of the blue, and she jumped in startled reaction. 'I was in Reception earlier,' he explained, his mouth twisting a little. 'I saw you with the baby. It's been a day of them, hasn't it?'

She didn't answer. She turned her head away from him, and he said, his tone sardonic, 'If you feel that way, why don't you hurry Matthew a little? Get him to name the day? You've been together for quite a while now, haven't you? Or doesn't he want children? Is that the problem?'

'Go away,' she said bluntly. 'I don't want to talk to you. Just leave me alone, get out of here, and mind your own damn business.'

'Tetchy, aren't we?' he murmured. 'Maybe you should see someone about that. Talk it through.'

'I don't need your advice,' she said tersely. 'Save it for your patients. I'm sure they'll welcome it.'

She thought he was going to argue with her, and her fingers tightened in her lap, her nails biting into her palms. But he didn't argue, just studied her silently for a moment, then turned and walked briskly back towards the centre.

It was almost three weeks later when he came by the flat. It was early evening, and Jessica was curled up in a chair reading a novel without making much headway, when she heard the ring at the door.

When she saw him standing there she was lost for words for the moment. She simply stared at him. Then, 'Nick,' she said. 'What are you doing here?'

'I've just come from Gemma's house. I heard you'd been visiting her and I thought we might talk about her for a while. There are so many interruptions at the centre, I thought I'd stop by here on the off chance you'd be in. Am I disturbing you? Were you in the middle of something?' He didn't ask if she had anyone with her, but it was there, hanging in the air between them.

'You'd better come in,' she said, moving to one side to let him through. 'I was reading. Science fiction, but I can't follow all the technical jargon. I'm about halfway through and I'm completely lost. I think I'll give the rest of it a miss.'

'That sounds like the best thing to do.'

She took him through to the sitting-room. 'Can I get you a drink? Coffee, or something stronger?' To her own ears, her voice sounded formal and ultra-polite, but there wasn't a thing she could do to change it.

'Nothing, thanks. I'm on call, so I have to keep a clear head.' He glanced around the room, his gaze flitting over the well-stocked book shelves, and coming to rest on the sideboard, where a silver trophy glinted in the light from a nearby lamp. 'A rugby trophy?' he murmured. 'Matthew's, obviously, unless you've taken to the sport recently.' He sent her an obliquely cynical look and she responded with a frosty glare. 'Matthew's, then,' he confirmed. 'Is he staying here now? Just not at home this evening?'

She sent him an icy look. 'I thought you came here to talk about Gemma?'

'So I did.' He sat down on the softly cushioned settee and she took a seat opposite him, sitting straight-backed and stiff with tension.

'So, what's happened?' she asked. 'Is Gemma OK? Has something happened to her? She seemed all right when I visited a few days ago—still depressed, but otherwise she seemed fine.'

'I'm afraid she's developed another bad dose of peritonitis since you last saw her. It's set her back quite a bit.'

'Oh, the poor little thing. . .' Jessica stood up and began to pace the floor. 'No wonder she keeps feeling so low.'

'She's responding to treatment well enough. I called in to check on her this evening, and she's showing signs of improvement, but, as you say, the depression is something else we have to deal with. What she really needs, of course, is a transplant, but until that becomes a possibility we have to help her adjust to the way things are now.'

Jessica went over to the sideboard. Absently, she stared down at the trophy for a moment or two, then she turned to face him again, her hands settling restlessly on the wooden surface behind her.

'The trouble is,' she muttered, 'she's very introspective at the moment. That's not altogether unnatural. Going back to school ought to have helped her come out of it, but instead it brought out more problems.'

'She's talked to you about this?'

'A little.' She pushed herself away from the sideboard. 'Children can be very cruel, especially if they see that someone is different from them and they don't understand the reasons for it. I think Gemma's suffering at the moment because she hasn't learned yet how to explain what's happened to her. She wants to be the same as everyone else, and she can't come to terms with being different.'

She walked over to the window and looked out at the field opposite. It was still light outside, and she could see the meadow grass and the sprawling, overgrown trees that made up the hedgerow. There was a peacefulness about nature that usually calmed her spirits, but today it would take more than that. She felt angry and tense; she wanted to rail at the unfairness of life.

'I agree. That's why I've an idea I want to put to you. I think we could try to do something to help.'

She swung around to face him again. 'Such as what?'

'Would you sit down? It might be easier for me to talk to you if you weren't pacing the room like a cat on hot bricks. What's the problem? Are you afraid Matthew might come home and find me here?'

Her mouth tightened. 'Of course I'm not afraid,' she snapped. 'Matthew won't be coming back here. He's studying for exams, he's very busy right now.'

'I see.' His gaze shifted to the rugby trophy and she felt her temper explode.

'Oh, for heaven's sake,' she burst out, 'I've had it engraved for him. I know someone who's very good at that sort of thing. Are you satisfied now? Can we get back to talking about Gemma? You had an idea you wanted to discuss?'

His wry smile maddened her even further. 'Am I touching on a nerve?' he murmured. 'I didn't mean to upset you.'

'You're not upsetting me,' she got out through her teeth. 'Just get on with what you had to say.'

He shrugged. 'I'm just trying to establish how we stand. I wish you would relax a little.'

She sat down with a thump. 'Is that better? You have my full attention.'

'Thanks.'

She was wearing a sleeveless silk blouse, and a smoothly fitting skirt, and his glance skimmed over her, coming to rest on the shapely length of her legs. She moved her hands restlessly, tugging the material of her skirt downwards.

He leaned forward and threaded his fingers lightly together, palms uppermost.

'I have a friend, a fellow doctor, who's established a residential centre on the south coast, not too far from Lulworth. It occurred to me that Gemma might benefit from spending some time there. It was set up for children like her, to give them a break and to help them meet and live with others in a similar situation to their own. I shall be going down there in a week or so. I've some leave due, and I promised Steve I'd stand in for him while he's away for a week. It seemed an ideal opportunity to suggest the idea of a visit to the Cresswells.'

Jessica nodded agreement. 'That sounds as though it might do some good. Will her parents be able to go, too?'

'Her father can't get time off work right now, but Mrs Cresswell is keen to go.'

'So, what's the problem?'

'Gemma,' he supplied drily. 'She won't hear of it. She doesn't want to go away from her familiar surroundings, and she doesn't think her mother really understands how she feels about everything. I think there's been a breakdown of communication somewhere along the line between the two of them.'

'That's difficult. They'd probably both benefit from the trip. It might alter their perspectives in some way.'

'That's what I thought. I've tried to persuade the girl to think again, but the only person she feels really comfortable with is you. I think if you were to go along with them she'd take to the idea.'

'Me?' She jumped up and started to pace again. 'Of course, I've grown very fond of Gemma, but how can I go? I have my work here; I can't just drop everything. And, anyway, you've already said you'll be there, so there shouldn't be any need for me to go along. You would be a familiar face for Gemma, and she likes you. She trusts you.'

'That's true. Unfortunately, it's you Gemma relates to most strongly. Probably because you're female, and you've done the renal training and you understand more what she's going through. You've been able to sympathise and offer support. It wouldn't take much to arrange, if you were to agree.'

'I—I don't know,' she said jerkily. 'I'm not sure. I'd have to think about it.'

'If you're concerned about taking time off, or losing some of your leave, I'm sure I could persuade Martyn to make a concession on that score. He's familiar with Gemma's case, and he's been very open to suggestions I've put to him.'

'You mean you've already discussed this with him?'

He shrugged. 'It came up in conversation. I'm bound to keep him in the picture. *Are* you worried about the question of leave?'

'No.' She walked to the window once more and stared out.

'Would Matthew object, is that it? Perhaps he wouldn't care for the two of us to spend time together?'

She didn't answer him, but continued to stare out at the landscape in front of her. It was getting dark now, it was harder to see, and the earlier brilliance of the colours was fading. There were shadows, and hidden places, and if a stranger looked out on that scene he wouldn't know what might be found out there.

That was how she felt. Nick was asking her to

go away from here, to unfamiliar territory, where, for a whole week they would be thrust into each other's company. She didn't know what would happen, or how she would feel, and it would be like stepping out into the unknown.

She felt a sudden chill, and wrapped her arms about herself, her hands chafing the bareness of her skin.

'What are you thinking, Jessica?' He came up behind her and placed his hands on her shoulders, turning her around to face him. 'Talk to me, don't try to shut me out, because I won't let you. Not any more.'

She said flatly, 'It's you I'm not sure about. I don't know what to expect from you any more. I hurt you once, and I'm sorry about that, but I don't think I'm prepared to go on paying for that for the rest of my life.'

He drew in a deep, sharp breath, and his hands tightened on her so that she could feel the tension in him. Then all at once the thread snapped, and she felt his grip ease and his thumbs begin to make slow circles on the vulnerable, smooth softness of her flesh, the warmth of his touch spreading widening ripples of answering sensation through all of her limbs.

'I understand that,' he said, and then suddenly released her, so that she felt lost all at once, bewildered and uncertain. 'There were loose threads for both of us,' he muttered, 'remnants of the past that hung about us, but you're right, that's all finished now. It's over and done with and we can put it behind us. I'd like you to come along on this trip, for Gemma's sake, but if you feel you can't do it then that's fine. I shan't mention it again.'

There was a chill ring of finality in his words that sent a small shiver through her body. He couldn't have made it more plain. His bitterness was spent. His love for her was gone along with it, finished, and she had only herself to thank for that. He was giving her the opportunity now to work alongside him, and he was doing it because he cared about little Gemma's happiness. The least she could do was to meet him in that challenge.

'I'll talk to Gemma,' she conceded. 'If she'll agree to go then I'll go along with her.'

# CHAPTER NINE

'ISN'T it breathtaking?' Jessica said, looking out from the window of her bedroom less than half an hour after they had arrived at Kingsland House. 'Just look at that view, Gemma. Have you ever seen anything so glorious?'

'I can see the bay from my room,' Gemma said. 'And the path down to the beach. I wanted to go down there straight away, but Mum absolutely insists we must unpack first. I'm supposed to be making a start on it now while she's on the phone to Dad.' She pulled a face and Jessica chuckled.

'Well, at least it will be one chore out of the way, and then you can concentrate on enjoying yourself for the rest of your time here.'

'I suppose so. Mum says she'll take me after lunch. Will you come with us?'

'Of course. I'm looking forward to exploring the place. There's a minibus on hand to take everyone out and about the rest of the week, did you know?'

'I know. Dr Tyler says I can do whatever I want, but I have to see him every morning for the all-clear, and again in the evening.'

'It shouldn't take up too much of your time. He's holding surgeries immediately after breakfast, and again after tea, just to check on medication, or deal with any problems that come up. Two of the children who'll be staying here are on CAPD just like yourself. I don't think they've arrived yet, but you'll probably meet up with them at teatime, and then you can get to know each other.'

'They might not want to talk to me,' Gemma said doubtfully.

'Oh, I'm pretty sure they will. They're not coming together, they're both from different parts of the country, and I expect they'll be feeling quite lost to begin with. You'll probably be able to make them feel more at home, since you arrived here first, and you know your way about a bit.'

Gemma nodded solemnly. 'I hadn't thought of that.'

She went out looking preoccupied, and Jessica decided it was time she made a start on her own unpacking. She pulled her case on to the divan and unlocked it. There wasn't anything really fancy in the case, since they were hardly likely to be socialising to any extent. It was mostly jeans and thin tops, with a couple of pairs of shorts and one or two sundresses added for good measure.

She was just hanging up the last garment in the wardrobe when there was a knock at the door, and she called out to whoever it was to come in.

Nick walked into the room. 'Are you about ready?' he asked. 'I've come to take you down to lunch.'

'Just about there.' She closed the wardrobe door and reached for a brush from the dressing-table, pulling it through her hair until she was satisfied that it had settled into its usual smooth style.

His glance followed her movements, flickering over the bright fall of burnished chestnut, before gliding down over her slender figure.

She was wearing a summery cotton print in shades of pink and gold. She liked the feel of it, the way it softly draped her hips and lightly swirled about her legs, but she wasn't sure what she felt when Nick looked at her that way. She couldn't read his expression; it was shuttered, his dark eyes glittering with some indefinable emotion, and that made her uncertain and a little edgy.

He came over to the window and looked out at the distant cliffs.

'What do you think of your room?' he asked, leaning back against the sill, one arm propped on the ledge. 'They're all very similar to this.'

'It's much larger than I expected, and much more luxurious than I'd imagined. Someone's gone to a lot of trouble to make sure everything blends perfectly. Look, there are even flowers on my table.'

A smile curved her lips as she bent a little to sniff the roses that had been made into a pleasing arrangement in a shallow ceramic bowl on the dressing-table.

'You haven't had much of a chance to see the rest of the place properly yet,' he said, 'but from what I've seen there have been a few additions since I was last down here. An indoor swimming pool and lounging area for a start.'

'I think it's wonderful,' Jessica said with enthusiasm. 'This house is so beautiful. There's not been much expense spared, has there? From what I've seen so far, there are all the facilities a disabled person might need—access for wheelchairs, handrails, lifts, even a stair lift. And as for the surroundings, they're lovely. You wouldn't even have to go out anywhere; you could stay right here in the grounds and feel really at peace with yourself.'

'I know what you mean. There's a gardener who makes sure everything is kept looking just right. He sees to it that there are plenty of flowers for the house throughout the year, and I believe there's a vegetable patch at the side so that we can reap the benefits of fresh produce. If the smells that were drifting from the kitchen just now are anything to go by I think we can look forward to some good meals while we're here.'

'You won't want to be going back to Soar Bridge, then, will you?' Jessica grinned. 'Your stomach was always your Achilles heel. Anything anyone wants, they only have to talk food, food, and more food, and it's theirs.' Not that he ever put on any weight. He was always far too active for that to happen, she thought.

'Not true,' he murmured, shaking his head. '*Delicious*, *well-cooked* food is the key.'

'That rules me out, then,' she said with an exaggerated sigh. 'I get by with a "how to boil water" cookbook.'

His gaze darkened momentarily and she silently cursed herself for her thoughtless remark, for unwittingly dragging up the past. But then his glance shifted obliquely and he said casually, 'I think I remember. Maybe it's a good thing some men take an interest in what goes on in the kitchen. Left to your tender mercies they might well starve.'

Her heart gave a little lurch. He'd said something like that once before, but he'd said it in fun, with a wryly amused glance in her direction before he'd taken over. There had been so many happy times, times when they had laughed together over her culinary efforts, and now the memories threatened to crowd in on her so that she had to struggle to push them away.

'Nonsense,' she said determinedly, putting down the brush. 'I know very well how to use a can opener, and the microwave's a doddle. Failing that, there's always the take-away.'

'So when you were holding forth to one of our patients about being self-sufficient, it was a case of do as I say, not as I do?' His mouth twisted. 'I think I'm being taken for a ride here. Shall we go down to lunch? If nothing else, you might pick up some tips.'

He dodged her light side-swipe, and they took the wide stairs down to the dining-room. There was no sign yet of Gemma or her mother, and they found a quiet table by the window where they could look out over the paved terrace with its burgeoning tubs of scarlet geraniums and striped petunias.

'I thought Gemma was looking better than she did a couple of weeks ago,' Jessica murmured. 'Is she fully recovered from the peritonitis now?'

'It looks that way,' Nick answered. 'We've everything we need here if any problems should develop, and the hospital's only fifteen minutes' drive away.'

'That's a relief, at any rate. Will you be on call twenty-four hours a day, or is there someone else on stand-by?'

'I'll have a couple of free nights, but there's always a number I can ring if things get hectic. It isn't likely to happen, though. The children are all fairly stable at the moment, with varying degrees of disability. There's good nursing back-up too. What I'd most like from this week is for Gemma to adjust to her condition, and realise that she's not on her own. I think you'll be a great help in that.'

'I can only try,' Jessica said. 'We're off to the beach this afternoon. Perhaps some of the other children will have had the same idea and she can meet up with them.'

Five days later it was becoming clear that their scheme was working. They were all assembled in the courtyard in front of the house, and Jessica gave a satisfied little smile as she watched Gemma excitedly boarding the minibus with her new-found friends. She was coming out of her shell nicely.

Jessica climbed on to the bus and took a seat near to the front. Mrs Cresswell passed her and went to sit next to her daughter, and the two of them started up a lively conversation. They were getting on much better these days, and that was another thing to be thankful for.

Nick slid into the seat beside her, checking his jacket pocket for his mobile phone, then deciding to take it off and consign both to the overhead rack.

'We've a scorching day ahead of us,' he murmured. 'Just the thing for a trip to the seaside. Have you ever been to Weymouth?'

She shook her head. 'No, have you? I've been abroad more than I've been to places in the British Isles,' she murmured with a twinge of regret. 'I shall have to remedy that. I've missed out on my heritage, in a way, though my parents were very fond of the Isle of Wight, and we've been there a few times.'

She looked up as the driver said something, checking that they were all safely on board. After a second or two he started up the engine and they were off, and all the children cheered.

'We went to Weymouth two or three times when I was a child,' Nick said, 'and I went again last year. I think you'll like it.'

She sent him a sideways glance. He looked relaxed, more so than she'd seen him in a long time, and she guessed that coming down south had done him quite a bit of good.

He was dressed casually in cool-looking fawn trousers and an open-necked shirt, and his skin was lightly tanned, contrasting warmly with the pale material of the shirt. Her glance rested fleetingly on the strong column of his throat, before she dragged it away. That was dangerous ground. She had to keep her mind free from the magnetic tug of her senses or she would surely be lost.

'It'll be a lovely experience for the children,' she murmured, pulling her thoughts back on track. 'Gemma's doing well, isn't she?' She kept her voice low so that no one but Nick would hear above the drone of the bus. 'She's found a friend who lives less than ten miles away from her, so with a bit of luck and cooperation on the part of both families they'll be able to meet up once they're back home.'

'I was hoping they'd get on well together. It looks as though they've clicked. Of course, they've a lot in common now, with CAPD.'

Jessica studied him thoughtfully a while. 'Did you have something to do with the bookings?' He shifted uncomfortably without answering and she went on quietly, 'I thought so. I thought it was odd that two children who lived so close should both be staying at the house the same week. I might have known you'd have fixed it that way. I should have remembered you don't like to leave things to chance.'

'I wasn't absolutely sure it would work out that way. I put out feelers, and they were taken up. There was no guarantee it would work, of course, but they do seem to have hit it off, and Gemma's becoming much more outgoing.'

'She's discovering what she can do, and what she can't,' Jessica agreed, 'and she's gradually gaining confidence, becoming more independent.'

She ought to have known he'd do the background research, checking up on other cases in the area. He wasn't just a doctor who did the job expected of him. If it was humanly possible he would always go that one step further.

The knowledge made her feel somehow. . . effervescent, charged with love and longing. She wanted to put her arms around him and hug him to her, to show him just how much she loved him. . . A faint tremor ran through her body. . . that would never do, would it?

Instead, she turned her gaze to the window and watched the landscape passing by, and for the rest of the journey kept up a desultory conversation with him that was strictly impersonal.

They arrived at their destination in good time. They stopped first at the sea-life park, where the children let off steam for a while on the wide expanse of grass before they went to see what else was on offer. A couple of hours later they left the minibus to make its own way and took the brightly coloured road train into town.

It was heartwarming, seeing the children's happy expressions; it made it all worthwhile. They had lunch in a café overlooking the sea, and then gathered up their belongings and went down to spend some time on the beach.

The sun was hot, and Jessica checked that everyone had put on a good layer of sunscreen before she went off to help some of the younger children build sandcastles. It was fun, but after a while she began to wilt in the heat, and settled back to watch the antics of the gulls searching for food along the shoreline.

'Shall we take a walk down to the old harbour?' Nick said after a time, and she stretched lazy limbs and wafted the front of her blouse to stave off the heat.

'That sounds like a good idea. I think I'm beginning to take root here.'

'That would never do. The tide might wash you away.' He pulled her to her feet, and while she brushed sand off her legs and slid her feet into sandals he went to tell everyone what they were planning on doing.

'Just you and me,' he said, coming back. 'No one wants to move. Gemma and her mates are looking for shells to take back home, and the Jenkins family are thinking of going round the shops. Jamie's parents are queuing up to hire a pedal boat. I don't think we'll be missed for a while. They know where to find us, anyway—I've said we'll be in the square not far from where the bus is to pick us up—and the nurses will bleep me if I'm needed.'

They took a leisurely walk down to the quayside and looked at the ships that were docked there, taking photos for the album. To get across the water to the old harbour they decided to take a ferry boat, rather than walk all the way around by the bridge.

It was a simple row boat that held fewer than ten people at a time, and when it pulled up alongside he helped her down the steps and into the rocking craft. It was cramped, and he put his arm around her waist, drawing her closer to him along the bench seat to make room as more people stepped down and the boat swayed on the water. His touch was strong and firm, making her skin heat and her blood swirl in fiery torment. She'd have liked to stay locked with him that way for evermore, but the journey was over too soon, and when they stepped out on to the far quay she felt odd all at once, as though part of her was missing.

'If we walk on a bit further,' he told her, 'we'll come to the square. There are lots of bars and shops, so, if you want to take back any souvenirs, now's your chance.'

'I'd like that. I want to pick up presents for

Mum and Dad while I'm here.'

The square wasn't at all what she'd expected. She'd thought of something modern, but this was cobbled, with quaint old fishing cottages all around, fronted with restaurants, cafés and bars. In the centre of the square a steel band was playing, not loud, raucous music, but a gentle, lilting rhythm that brought a smile to her lips. There were barbecues, too, the smell of charcoal mingling with hot onions and burgers and baked potatoes, and all around were tables and chairs, painted wooden ones, or plain white plastic, or ornately carved wrought iron, depending which café they fronted. Jessica stared about her, fascinated, taking everything in.

'I love it,' she breathed. 'I'd no idea this was hidden away, just around the corner.'

'Come and look at the shopping complex,' he said, 'and we'll come back here to relax when we've finished. It's worth a look around. It was built on the site of a Victorian brewery.'

It was a delightful shopping village. The original paved streets and courtyards had been left in place, and there were bow-fronted shop windows to draw the attention to the goods on display. There were all kinds of shops under one roof. Nick helped her choose gifts, some beautiful tinted glassware for her mother, and a tooled leather writing case for her father. There was a shop in there where they were selling hand-crafted wooden toys, and Nick bought something for each of his nieces and nephews.

When they went out into the sunlit cobbled square once more the smell of barbecued food drifted across to them and tantalised her nostrils. She must have tilted her nose in appreciation because he laughed and said, 'Are you hungry? Find a table for us over there and I'll get some drinks and something to eat.'

The band was still playing as they ate, and Jessica thought wistfully how romantic it was, sitting here with him, enjoying a cool drink in the warmth of the late afternoon. Funny how deceptive appearances could be.

'You said you came here last year,' she murmured, trying to quell any betraying note in her voice. 'Was that with your family, or shouldn't I ask?'

His mouth moved in a wry smile. 'You can ask. As a matter of fact I came with my cousin Chris. We were here to see the ships at the start of the tall ships' race. At night there was a torchlight procession across the beach and a firework display out over the water, with searchlights beaming out to pick up the masts. Then in the morning the ships paraded across the bay in full sail before heading off towards Plymouth. It was a sight to see. You'd have loved being there.'

'Yes,' she said quietly, 'I'm sure I would,' and hoped he would put the faint huskiness of her voice down to a dryness in her throat. She sipped at her drink.

'Where did you go?' he asked, and she looked up at him quickly, her gaze questioning, so that he added drily, 'With Matthew? You *did* have a holiday last year, didn't you?'

She floundered for a moment, then said offhandedly, 'Of course. Our dates didn't coincide, though. I'd started this new job at the health centre, and there was the rota to consider. . . Matthew's grandfather was very ill, and he spent a lot of his leave with him. I went to stay with my aunt Becky. She lives near here, actually—well, nearer to Lulworth. I was hoping I might get the chance to go over and see her while I'm down here, but I'm not sure about transport. I don't know if there's a coach that goes that way——'

'Of course you should visit her. I could drive you if you wanted—I'm free tomorrow evening. Unless you'd rather go alone?'

'No, I—that is, it would be good if you could come along. I'm sure Becky would love to meet you. She missed the engagement party and. . .' Her voice trailed off and she went hot all over as she realised she'd done it again. It was bad enough when Nick brought up the past, but she was adding to it, and there was no way she could skirt around it now. 'Well, she always used to ask about you, and she still mentions you in her letters from time to time. Mum always thought the world of you, and she passed that on to Becky, so Becky feels she missed out. She hates what she calls unfinished business.'

'We can't have that, can we?' he said crisply, glancing at his watch. 'It's time we were making a move. The bus will be waiting to take us back.'

'I suppose you're right. Nick—about Becky. . . she's a bit. . .well, forthright, I suppose. I love her dearly, and I'm used to her ways, but you——'

He raised a brow. 'I see nothing wrong with being forthright, and, anyway, I'm not made of jelly. She isn't likely to cause me any problems I can't handle.' Getting to his feet, he added, 'You could give her a ring when we get to the house and see if tomorrow's OK for a visit.'

'I will.'

The earlier mood was lost, and they walked to the bus in virtual silence. On the drive back to the house Nick produced an electronic notebook and soon became engrossed in dealing with various entries. Jessica looked out of the window and watched the scenery passing by.

Gemma caught her attention after a few minutes, when she had been in danger of drifting into hopeless dreaming, building castles in the air. Excitedly the child pointed out the huge figure of a horse and rider carved out of the chalk hillside, and Jessica straightened up in her seat and said, 'It's supposed to be King George III. I think I read somewhere that it's almost three hundred feet long, and over three hundred feet high. It looks magnificent, doesn't it?'

Becky wasn't in when she phoned later, but Uncle Jack took a message and said they'd love to see her and whoever she cared to bring along. They'd have a tipple, he said, and Becky would produce some of her home-baked cookies.

'He's a coastguard,' Jessica told Nick. 'He says a drop of whisky keeps out the cold.'

'I expect it does.'

He was off duty from about four o'clock next day, and they set off straight away, heading towards Lulworth. They stopped for a while to take tea in a small café, then explored the area around the cove. They stood on a promontory, high above the sea, and looked down at the cliffs and the fascinating rock formations, watching the sea eddy about making lacy splashes of white foam.

After a minute or two Jessica drew back, stumbling a little, and Nick's arm came around her waist, steadying her.

'I get dizzy,' she explained breathlessly, 'looking down from this height. I feel as though I'm going to sway, and topple over.'

'I shan't let you do that,' he murmured. 'Trust me.'

She did trust him; she would trust him with her life. So she leaned back into the protective shelter of his arms and watched the waves pounding the rocks while her heart thundered and echoed the crashing beat.

They stayed there for some time, but when more people came to look at the view Nick said, 'Becky will be waiting,' and led her away towards the car.

Jack met them at the door of the house. He gave her a big hug and shook hands with Nick, then took them inside. It was a lovely old cottage, white-painted, with a long sloping roof and tiny windows set into the eaves.

Jack had to stoop a little to miss one of the crooked, low door frames. He was a tall man, strongly built, with greying hair and clear blue eyes. His skin was weathered, from long hours out at sea, and there were deep crease lines in his cheeks, mostly put there by smiles, Jessica thought. She had always liked him; he was a very peaceful man.

'Becky's just cleaning up,' he said, then

laughed. 'Not the house—herself. You know what she's like, don't you, Jess? Out all day with her paints and canvas. She's a lot like your mother. . . once she gets absorbed in her painting she forgets everything. Not today, mind. It's just taking her longer than usual to get the paint off her fingers.'

'My aunt paints landscapes,' Jessica explained to Nick. 'She's very talented. The gallery in the village displays them, and she makes some good sales.'

'She does portraits, too, sometimes,' Jack said, 'but she prefers landscapes. It's not exactly a living, but then, a lot of good artists have to be dead before they're recognised.' He chuckled at that. 'She did a painting of our Jess one time when she came for a visit. It's a wild scene, out on the cliff top, and the wind was blowing something fierce. It's good, very good, but she won't let that one go, sentimental old stick.'

Jessica hadn't known what Becky was doing until after the painting was complete. She must have done it all from sketches, from times when they'd walked the hills together and she'd poured out her heart to her that lonely, terrible winter. She wasn't going to think about that now.

'Come out to the terrace,' Jack said, 'and sit down while I go and sort out some drinks. I'll show you round the garden later. Are you a gardening man?' he said to Nick.

'I might be when I get the chance,' Nick answered obliquely. 'I've still to find the right house, but I do want a big garden, I know that much.' He glanced around admiringly. 'This one looks like something out of *Homes and Gardens*.'

Jack looked pleased. 'I put up a pergola down the bottom end in the spring and there are one or two nice ramblers you might like to see. I've been trying to establish an espalier apple, but this is the first year I've had much success.'

'Is he going on about his garden again?' Becky said with a chuckle, coming out to meet them. She had strong, waving brown hair, with a few streaks of grey here and there, and her eyes were sparkling brown. Her hands were long-fingered, capable-looking, and there wasn't a speck of paint left on them.

Jack went off in search of drinks, while Becky flung her arms around Jessica and hugged her close. 'It's good to see you again, my love.'

Standing back, she turned to Nick. 'Thanks for bringing her. Jack will pin your ears back over the garden, you know. I hope you won't mind. It's his pride and joy, and he's reason enough to be pleased with himself, because it is looking its best right now, I must admit. He likes it to look good all year round, and mostly it does—though it was a bit bleak when Jess came to see us the other winter, what with all the wind and rain. Everything looked so bedraggled—he was heart-broken. Not that Jess noticed. She was too ill to worry much about that, and what with breaking up with her young man and all, it wasn't a very good time. I told her then——'

'Aunt Becky——' Jessica cut in, a small frown working its way between her brows, and Becky threw her hands up in the air in a haphazard gesture.

'I'm doing it again, aren't I? Letting my tongue

run away with me. Of course your friend here doesn't want to listen to me rattling on about that.' She walked over to the patio table and picked up a plate of cookies. 'Perhaps I should munch on one of these. It's the only way. . . Come and hand out serviettes, will you?'

Jessica managed a faint smile, and went to do as she was bid. Nick had taken up a position against the wall of the house, leaning negligently, his arms folded casually across his chest. There was nothing casual about his expression, though. It was steadily watchful, so that as she walked to the table she almost faltered under the brooding darkness of his eyes.

'Cookies,' Becky said, brandishing the plate. 'Now then, young man, get one of these down you and tell me all about yourself. You're in charge of things down at the house for the week, aren't you?'

'Becky,' Jessica said awkwardly, 'this is Nick. Nick Tyler. Didn't Uncle Jack tell you?'

'Oh, Lord,' Becky said, swinging her glance from one to the other and back again to Nick. 'So you're the one. Are you two back together again? I told Jess she was making a mistake at the time, but she wouldn't have it. Nice upstanding man like yourself. I know all about you, you know. I heard it from her mum. But I mustn't ramble on, must I?' She sighed and flicked her gaze to Jessica. 'No, love, he didn't tell me. You know your Uncle Jack, always has his mind up in the clouds.'

'Am I in trouble again?' Jack queried, coming out of the conservatory with a bottle and peering at the label. 'What have I done this time? Does anyone fancy a glass of parsnip wine, vintage '91? It's Becky's handiwork, not mine, so I can't vouch for it.' He pulled the cork, sniffing at the rim of the bottle, and Becky thumped him lightly on the arm.

They stayed until it grew dark, and on the whole the evening was a success. Jessica was thankful that Becky restrained herself from commenting any more on the relationship between herself and Nick. She'd been on a bit of a knife edge after that first blunder, but she'd explained they were just working together now, and for once Becky had held back, so that after a while she had been able to relax.

Later on in the evening Becky took Nick to look round what she called her studio, while Jessica stayed behind in the sitting-room and talked to Jack and drank more of the parsnip wine, until she felt pleasantly sleepy.

'They're a nice couple,' Nick said when they were driving home. 'She must miss your mother, with them living so far apart.'

'She does, but Uncle Jack has to stay here—it's where his livelihood is. They write to each other, of course, and phone regularly. Martyn has the same difficulty with his parents, doesn't he, with them living on the coast?'

'That's true. Do your aunt and uncle live alone? Is there any family round about?'

'No, there's just the two of them.'

'They seem very well suited.'

'They do, don't they?'

He drew the car to a halt outside the house,

and Jessica stretched a little before climbing out on to the tarmac.

'Fancy a nightcap before turning in?' Nick asked. 'There's a bottle of brandy in the study I wouldn't mind a shot at.'

'Brandy and parsnip? Why not?'

She walked with him to the dimly lit house and into the study. The house was quiet, and she said in a low voice, 'Everyone must have gone to bed. I hadn't realised it was quite so late.'

He switched on the table lamp and went over to the cabinet, gently clinking bottles and glasses. Jessica found the buttoned couch and sat down on it, tipping her head back against the soft leather. She was feeling tranquil, relaxed, warm from the wine she had drunk earlier, though Nick hadn't had much, she'd noticed, since he was driving.

He came and sat next to her, passing her a brandy liqueur which he knew was her favourite. She sipped it, tasting the sweetness on her lips with the tip of her tongue, while he swirled his own drink gently, staring down at the amber liquid in his glass before tilting it to his mouth and drinking it in one long swallow.

She watched him, absorbed in the movement of his throat, in the texture of his skin. She could feel the warmth emanating from his body, he was so close, and his arm brushed hers as he moved to put the glass down on the table.

'Don't look at me like that,' he said.

'Why?' She couldn't drag her gaze from him; she wanted to drink him in.

'Because when you look at me like that it makes

me lose control,' he muttered, reaching over to take the liqueur glass from her and put it next to his. He moved closer, gently edging her back against the cushions of the couch. 'It makes me want to kiss you. And you wouldn't want that, would you? Would you?' His mouth touched hers, the lightest, merest touch, and he whispered, 'But you'll have to tell me, you'll have to make me know it for sure, because I don't think I want to stop.'

She didn't want him to stop. His lips enticed her, drew her to cling to him in eager response so that his arms closed round her and she knew that soon there would be no going back.

His mouth crushed hers, and she tasted the brandy on his lips, swallowed his muttered words with her own hungry kisses. She had crossed over the threshold between sanity and desire, and all she could think of was the joy it gave her to give herself up to his caresses, to run her hands over his chest, his arms, and feel the strength in him. Their bodies tangled, wrapped together in heated passion, and she trembled with fierce longing, aching to be part of him, to draw him into her soul. It was all she had ever wanted, and she was tired of denying herself this one expression of her love, of denying him.

She ran her finger lightly along his jaw, delicately exploring his bone structure, delighting in the feel of his firm skin beneath her fingertips.

'Jessy?' His stroking hand moved over her breast, her ribcage, slid possessively down over the curve of hip and thigh. 'I want you. . . I've never stopped wanting you, you know that, don't you? You tantalise me; you make me ache with wanting. . .'

Temptation soared within her, the blood pounding in her ears until it made her head buzz. She needed him—why shouldn't she take what he offered, a few moments of closeness, of sharing, of belonging to each other? Would that be so bad?

'Jessy?' he said again, and she looked up into his eyes and saw the darkness there, and knew that she couldn't bear to hurt him again. She wanted him so much, it would be so easy, so simple just to push the world away and pretend nothing else existed.

But there would always be the aftermath, the awful time of truth, and then the long, slow falling apart of all they had ever had.

'This is madness,' she whispered. 'I shouldn't be here; this shouldn't be happening.'

He started to speak, and she touched her finger to his mouth, stemming the words. 'I'm not thinking straight,' she said huskily. 'My mind's hazy with drink, or I wouldn't have let this happen. I'm sorry, I'm so sorry. But you and me. . .it isn't possible, it just isn't possible.'

He gripped her fingers, pressing her hand back against the couch. 'Why?' he muttered harshly. 'Tell me why.'

'You know the reasons,' she said, her voice breaking. 'What we had before, it all came apart. . .there isn't any going back, there can't be.'

'Because of Matthew?' His lowered tones were shot through with barely contained anger. He shifted away from her, his movements jerky, his whole body stiffening. 'He came into your life, and everything that went before it was swept away as though it had never existed. But where is he now? Where has he been this last year? I don't see him racing to put a ring on your finger. And how many times has he called you since we arrived here? I'll tell you—not once. We've been here almost a week, and he hasn't phoned once. That strikes me as odd, Jessica; that doesn't strike me as the kind of relationship that's going anywhere. I want an explanation, I want to know what the hell's going on.'

She sat bolt upright, nervously smoothing down the crumpled folds of her skirt. 'I don't have to explain anything.'

'You want me,' he said tersely. 'I'm not blind, or stupid, or without sensitivity. I know that you want me, but you say there's no place for me in your life. So where does that leave me? What am I supposed to think about that? That things between you and Matthew have cooled and you were feeling a little frustrated, and I just happened along? Isn't it time you told me the truth?'

'I told you the truth,' she said hoarsely. 'I had too much to drink and I wasn't thinking straight, or this would never have happened at all. I'm sorry.' She got to her feet and dragged in a shuddery breath, her fingers twining and twisting with all the tension that was pent up inside her. 'I've said I'm sorry, and I mean it, but I can't go on saying it. I *won't* go on saying it. I don't want to talk about this any more. I'm going to bed. I didn't mean to cause you pain, but I'm all through, I can't cope any more, and you have to deal with your emotions your own way.'

He stared at her, his mouth hard. 'I shall, Jessica. Run away if you will, but this is not the end of it. You've blown hot and cold for too long now, and I've taken as much wavering from you as I'm prepared to. From now on I *shall* deal with this my way, you can count on that.'

## CHAPTER TEN

NICK had said he was going to deal with it, and Jessica didn't know quite what he meant by that. In any case, she couldn't afford to let it bother her. Once back at the health centre, the days were full enough, with staff going down with a stomach bug and calling in sick, and the workload varying according to whether or not temps could be found. She didn't mind any of it. She was glad to keep busy. It stopped her from thinking about other things.

Nick had changed, somehow. She couldn't quite pin down what it was about him, because his manner was as civil as ever to everyone he came into contact with. He worked hard, as usual, and he was as decisive as before. But towards herself. . .there was a firmness in his manner, a sharpness in the way he looked at her that made her check everything she'd done and then check again. It was unnerving, unsettling.

The seasons were changing again, the days were getting cooler, and just lately a portion of her time was taken up in dealing with people, children especially, suffering the results of cold viruses. She found herself giving out general advice, or sending patients on to be seen by the doctors.

Nick came into the treatment-room one day when she was syringing a child's ears, and he waited until she had finished, reading through the leaflets on display.

'All done,' she told the boy. 'You should be able to hear much better now.'

She showed him out, then started to clear everything away, more slowly than usual because these last few days her pains were back, stronger than they'd been before, and she was trying to control them with deep breathing and careful movements.

Nick glanced at her, his eyes narrowing a little, but he made no comment and she was glad of that. He slotted a leaflet back into the wire rack, and said, 'Gemma seems to be doing well since her visit to Kingsland House. Her mother's just been in for a chat, and it looks as though she's getting on much better at school now. She's being straightforward about her condition with anyone who asks, and her schoolwork's picking up. I think we did well to get her to go away.'

'I didn't have any doubts about that,' she murmured. 'Do you think there'll be any chance of a transplant in the near future?'

'It's hard to say. The family are undergoing tests, but we don't know yet what the outcome will be.'

'She has a brother and sister, doesn't she?'

'That's right. The boy's studying for his A levels, and the sister has just finished university. She wasn't sure whether to stay on for another year, or try for a job.'

'They're not always easy to come by these days, even for graduates.' She turned to put a kidney dish away in the cupboard, and a spasm of pain made her still for a moment. Then, as the spasm died away, she added, 'I'm glad I'm not in the job market. It can't be any fun.'

Nick took the dish from her hand and placed it on the shelf. 'Sarah was right,' he said crisply. 'You should get a second opinion about that problem of yours. It's more than just the odd twinge, and it's gone on for far too long.'

'And how would you know about that?' she queried, her tone dismissive. 'I've never said that it was anything more than a few natural aches and pains, no more than most women get from time to time.'

'Becky told me. She said it was more than that. That you sometimes suffered badly.'

Jessica gasped. 'She had no right. How could she do that? I can't believe she would say anything that——' She broke off in agitation, wondering just what it was that Becky had said. Then her head cleared a little as she thought things through. Becky was bound to secrecy. She knew how much it meant to Jessica to keep the truth from Nick, and even if she didn't agree with her reasoning she surely wouldn't betray her trust. 'What did she say to you?'

'When we first met she said you had been ill that winter when you visited, and later on I asked her about it. She was very cagey at first, but I wasn't inclined to leave it be. You'd been to your doctor, she said, and then she shut up like a clam.' His gaze was darkly probing. 'Whatever you've been told, it needs further investigation. Do you want me to check you over? I could refer you on to someone, if need be.'

'No—certainly not.' She went hot all over at

the very thought, and her words came out more sharply than she'd intended. 'I don't know why you're making such an issue out of this. I haven't asked for your help, or Sarah's, and I can manage perfectly well, thank you.'

His mouth tightened. 'For heaven's sake, Jessica, I'm a doctor. If there's something wrong with you——'

'There is nothing wrong with me. Leave me be.' She pulled open a drawer and began to search inside it for her notepad, anything to keep busy, to keep him from prying further.

'If you don't want me to look at you then go to Sarah. I'll speak to her about it——'

'You'll do no such thing,' she said tersely. 'Don't you *dare* do anything of the sort.' She pushed the drawer shut with a lot more firmness than was necessary, and went over to the computer. 'I've some work to do,' she muttered. 'Haven't you?'

'I never realised before just how stubborn you can be,' he said abrasively, his eyes glittering like polished steel. 'In fact, I would never have said it was a trait in you.'

'Then you've learned something new, haven't you?' She half turned away from him and fed a disk into the computer.

He walked out without another word, but his expression was grim and she bit her lip and put her mind to typing up her notes.

It was her birthday a few days later, on the Saturday, and, since she didn't have to work, she planned a lie-in, with a leisurely bath to follow. She'd already received parcels from her parents and her sister, Suzy, and several of her friends had dropped by last night for a cheerful get-together. The wine glasses were still in the sink where she'd left them. She'd gone to bed full of alcohol and nibbles, and she was amazed to find that her head was clear when she woke several hours later. There'd be another party tonight with the family, at her parents' home, and she was looking forward to it.

The phone rang, and she reached out a hand to the bedside table, yawning, and chatted with her mother for a while, until thoughts of a lie-in slowly began to recede. Her mother was always an early riser, hating to miss out on any part of the day. Jessica stretched lazily. Perhaps she'd make a cup of tea, ease herself into things gradually.

The doorbell sounded next, and she gave a rueful smile. So much for plans. . .

It was Nick. She stared at him, a batch of envelopes in her hand, hastily scooped up from the doormat.

'What are you doing here?' she asked, frowning. 'It's not even—' she broke off to glance at the clock '—eight-thirty yet.'

'I take it you're alone?' he said. 'There's no car in your space downstairs.'

She stiffened, her chin lifting. 'And if I am?'

Her cool demeanour did nothing to put him off. Instead there was a satisfied gleam in his eyes and a faint curve to his mouth.

'You haven't eaten yet?' he wanted to know, his gaze warmly skimming her shapeliness, her feminine curves revealed by the loose robe she wore, so that she pulled the edges of it together with her free hand, scrunching the silk in her palm.

She frowned. 'No. Why do you ask?'

'Good. I didn't think you would have, not on your day off. I thought we'd have breakfast together. Aren't you going to invite me in?'

He stepped into the hall and she moved to one side, closing the door behind him with a bewildered expression.

'Perhaps I'm not fully awake yet,' she said, 'but I'm confused. Do you think you could explain? You don't usually visit at this hour of the day.'

'True. There's nothing like breaking the mould, is there? I thought I'd make breakfast for us, since you're not at your best with a frying-pan. Then I hope you'll forget whatever plans you had for the morning, since I have something in mind for us.'

'I was planning,' she told him frostily, 'on spending a good part of the morning in bed.'

'Really?' His mouth made a devilish curve. 'Well. . .maybe I could rethink. Your idea sounds pretty good to me. We could always eat later.'

His fingers went to the collar of his shirt, but before he could tug a button free she said huskily, 'Stop playing games, Nick, and tell me why you're here.'

He laughed, and there was a mocking glint in his eyes that was infinitely disturbing. 'Nervous, Jessica?'

'Certainly not,' she muttered crossly, denying the crazy leap of her pulse, and taking refuge in putting the envelopes on the hall table. Her fingers shook a little, and she hoped he wouldn't notice. 'I wish you would be sensible and tell me what brings you here.'

'I found a house,' he said. 'I'd like you to come with me to look at it.' He walked into the kitchen and she followed him, watching bemusedly as he started opening doors and drawers until he found a frying-pan and various other cooking utensils. 'Happy birthday, by the way.' He straightened and pulled a soft package from his pocket, handing it to her. 'A present for you.'

She held it, looking at him wordlessly until he said, 'Open it. I didn't buy it so it could stay in the wrapping.'

She did as she was told, and as the scraps of silk and lace came into view he said, 'I hope they fit. If memory serves me right they should. I'd suggest you try them on now, and let me see for myself, but I expect that would be pushing my luck too far. I'll do my best to imagine what they look like instead.'

Hot colour washed along her cheek bones as she fingered the delicately fashioned lingerie. 'They're beautiful,' she whispered, and felt a little choked. It was the loveliest set of underwear she'd ever seen, and every time she wore it she would think of him. Perhaps that was what he wanted.

She swallowed hard and tried to gather her wandering thoughts. 'I'm glad you found a house,' she said. 'But why do you need me to go with you? Can't you make up your mind about it?'

'I'm fairly sure it's the one,' he said, tossing bacon into the pan and turning the gas down when it sizzled. He must have brought the food with him, though she'd been too dazed by his unexpected appearance to take note of what he'd been carrying. 'But I'd like a woman's opinion. You're very good at seeing possibilities, and you might notice something I've missed. Will you do it?'

'Of course.' She wanted, more than anything, to see his home, but the thought that he might be going to share it with someone else sent a chill quivering through her spine.

She tried not to think about that. Instead she watched him work, his movements efficient, his manner sure, as though he'd been around her kitchen for years. She felt very strange, as though none of this was happening, as though she was locked into a dream. 'What about Claire, though, or Jennifer?' she asked him. 'Wouldn't they have offered advice?'

He grinned at that. 'I expect they would. Lots of it. But actually Claire is on duty this weekend, and Jennifer's away.'

He dealt with the eggs, tapping them smartly and dropping them into the pan. 'Are you going to sit down and eat in your night things, or did you want to dress first?' His glance swept over her, and she realised hotly that the edges of the robe were coming apart again, to reveal the skimpy slip of satin she wore beneath it. 'Personally, I'd prefer you to stay like that,' he murmured, his mouth curving in a way that made her bones melt, 'but, if you did want to change, you'd better do it now, because this food will be ready before too long.'

His teasing made her heart begin to drum against her ribs with an erratic, jerky beat, and all the while his gleaming eyes were throwing out a challenge, making the blood rush to her head. It was too much, and she fled, shutting the bathroom door on the sound of his soft laughter.

The doorbell went again as she stepped out of the bath a few minutes later, and when she heard male voices she frowned, wondering who on earth that could be. She wrapped a towel around herself and ran her fingers through her hair, then put her head round the door.

If it was the milkman, standing in for the regular one, the bill had already been paid, and she didn't want Nick dipping into his pocket to pay him twice.

He was holding the front door slightly ajar, his arm and body partly blocking her view, but she managed to catch a glimpse of Matthew's familiar figure just as he was turning away.

'Matthew?' she said in surprise. She edged a little further out of the room, exposing a naked shoulder to the cooler air of the hall.

'Ah—I have to go,' Matthew said, giving her a faint smile and casting an odd look in Nick's direction. 'I'll catch you later, Jessica. I just came by to wish you a happy birthday.'

He gave a slight wave of his hand before moving away down the steps, and Nick shut the door firmly behind him.

'He must have been in a hurry,' he said, looking totally unconcerned. 'Don't feel too disappointed, will you?' he added grittily. 'I'm sure he would have stayed if he could.'

From a distance they heard Matthew's car growl into life and move off across the car park.

'I didn't even get the chance to speak to him,

to say hello,' Jessica bit out, letting go of the bathroom door to hitch up her towel. She glared at him. 'He never rushes off like that. You must have said something to him. He looked so. . .put out. What did you say to him?'

'Me?' He raised a brow. 'I just told him the truth, of course. That you were taking a bath, and we were about to have breakfast. What would you have me say to him?'

Her eyes narrowed. 'You made it sound as though something was going on between you and me,' she said abruptly. 'Why would you do that?'

'I only told him the truth. It's hardly my fault if he decides to draw his own conclusions.' He shrugged, his mouth twisting a little. 'He left some flowers for you. Very romantic.' His glance flicked to the bouquet of pink roses on the hall table, then moved back to slant over her scantily clad form. 'Maybe I should have delayed him, after all, if it was so important to you. Were you planning on entertaining him dressed like that?'

'What I do, or don't do, is none of your business,' she retorted sharply. 'And as to Matthew drawing conclusions, you're very fond of jumping to your own, aren't you?'

'And what's that supposed to mean?' His eyes glittered dangerously, and she began to wish she hadn't let her tongue run away with her.

'Nothing; it doesn't mean anything,' she faltered as he came towards her. 'It's just a statement of fact.' She backed away. 'I must get dressed.'

'What's the hurry?' he muttered. 'You weren't in such a hurry a moment ago.' His hand shot out to grip her wrist and tug her towards him. 'You know, I appreciate your beauty every bit as much as Matthew. More so. . .and I had prior claim. Maybe I should have made that clear from the outset; I shouldn't have given him the chance to muscle in. . .'

'I'm not some kind of shop goods that you can fight over,' she said shakily, struggling a little as he drew her against him. 'You can't treat me that way, I shan't let you. I have my own feelings and emotions, I have a free choice. . .'

His arms slid around her. 'But you're not thinking clearly, are you? You said so yourself once before.' He lowered his head towards her, gently rubbing her cheek with his own and gliding his lips warmly over the vulnerable place beneath the lobe of her ear. She trembled in startled response and caught her breath, all the struggle beginning to seep out of her. It wasn't fair, the way her treacherous body responded to him; she didn't have any defences against him.

His breath was warm against her throat, his voice roughened. 'You haven't been thinking clearly for a long while, and I think it's about time I helped you to sort out what it is you really want.'

His mouth trailed a warm path over her soft skin until he touched her lips with his own and nudged them apart, kissing her with a thoroughness that left her breathless and clinging to him in desperate need. His hands stroked her, sliding over every curve and valley, pressuring her to him, so that she couldn't help but feel the strength in him, and hear the heavy thud of his heart beating against hers. Her bare legs tangled with his, and heated sensation rippled through her nerve endings, coursing through her body until she felt weak and heady with desire.

'Nick,' she whispered, trying to break away before things raced out of control, her fingers curling into the thin material of his shirt.

His kisses muffled her words, and when his lips slid down over the arch of her throat, and lower, to taste the soft curve of her breast, she knew she was fighting a losing battle. Her fingers moved convulsively as his tongue made a slow, delicious sweep along her soft, sensitised flesh.

'You want me,' he murmured against the softness of her mouth. 'Tell me you want me.'

She registered the smooth ripple of his muscles beneath her fingers and felt the heat in him, and knew that she had no defence that would stop the treacherous melting of her limbs. He went to her blood faster than pure alcohol on an empty stomach, burning into her system, firing up her senses until there was nothing else, nothing but him.

'Tell me,' he said again.

Her mind spiralled dizzily, shooting off on a fantasy voyage, where anything was possible. . . they could belong to each other, and nothing could intrude on their bliss.

'I want you,' she whispered.

It was a dream, though, just a dream. She wanted it to go on forever, but it was an impossible dream and she had to wake from it. Some time she had to wake. She shook her head as though she could shake off the gossamer threads that were stopping her from thinking clearly. If only there was some way they could be together. . .'I want you,' she said, huskily, 'but——'

He put his finger to her lips to stem the words. 'There we have it. There's always a but, isn't there?' He looked down at her and there was a darkness about his eyes, a sudden harshness to his features that hadn't been there before. Then his mouth moved in a cynical smile, and he put her away from him, at arm's length, and she felt as though she had lost something so precious that it could never be replaced, and it made her want to weep with despair. 'You'd better get dressed,' he said coolly. 'Breakfast's been warming long enough, and I have to pick up the key to the house before ten.'

'Oh. . .yes.' She stumbled a little as she tried to move backwards, away from him. 'Of course, the house.' She had forgotten about that, she had been so carried away, but he hadn't let it slip his mind. There was always that cool part of his brain that registered other matters, and, perversely, she found herself resenting that.

She was confused by his abrupt change of mood, though she could hardly have expected anything else. He had said that she blew hot and cold, and she couldn't blame him for being irritated by that.

Even so, he was doing a fairly good imitation himself right now. Perhaps these last few minutes had meant nothing more to him than a way of salvaging his pride and putting his own virility to the test.

He had been filled with bitterness since Matthew had come into her life, and maybe this was his way of ridding himself of the cobwebs from the past. He had wanted to prove that he could have her, and they both knew in their heart of hearts that with very little persuasion on his part they could have been making love right now.

He hadn't pursued his goal further, though. He had achieved his aim well enough. He had made her admit to wanting him, and perhaps, all along, that was all he had really hoped to achieve.

He had lived a separate life from her for this last year and more. Why should he need her now? There must have been more than enough women willing to step into her shoes. She only had to listen to the muted conversations among the nurses in the staff lounge to know that.

He went off to the kitchen, and she hurried inside the bathroom to dress quickly in jeans and a snug-fitting cotton body. She'd said she would go with him to the house, and she had to see it through now, though the thought that he might be making a home for some other woman was almost more than she could bear.

Breakfast was an odd affair. Sitting across the table from the man she loved, knowing that he no longer wanted her, was an ordeal, and she was glad when it was over.

He had treated her as though their lovemaking had never happened, and had talked to her about this and that as though everything was normal. Nothing was normal as far as she was concerned. She was bewildered, distracted by her own fickle nature, filled with a conflicting upsurge of emotions that made her want to weep.

She kept back the tears, though, blinking away

the stinging of her eyelids and setting herself to the morning's visit with an open mind.

'Well, what do you think?' he asked when they arrived at the house some time later. 'It hasn't been lived in for a couple of months because the owners have been out of the country, and everything's been let to go a bit wild.'

That was true enough. The front garden sprawled untidily, with overgrown shrubs and clumps of bright flowers spreading over the curving path, but it simply added to the beauty of the place as far as Jessica was concerned. Just standing back and looking at the scene brought a lump to her throat.

'Perhaps it should be left just the way it is now,' she said. 'It looks as though years of love and attention have been lavished here. So many different flowers, peeping out where you wouldn't have expected them. I can imagine children playing in this garden, and it wouldn't matter a jot if they broke anything down, because something would always spring up to replace it.'

The house was built from warm tinted reddish stone, and a lot of the frontage was hidden by trellis work and shrubs that clambered in profusion over the wall, threatening to obscure some of the windows. They were large and square-latticed, and there was a deep slate roof from under which the bedroom windows peeped out. There were two chimneys, one in the centre and one at the side, that added character to the whole, and the front door was set back in a porch that was almost covered by a rambling pink japonica.

She didn't really need to see the inside. She

had already fallen in love with the house.

'I think,' she said, 'it was well worth waiting for. Is the rest of it as lovely?'

He was pleased by her comment. They walked through the various rooms, and she could see why he had chosen this house. The living-room was big and bright with patio doors that opened on to a weathered terrace. Beyond that, the garden sprawled, in the same way as the front, with trees and shrubs, and a summer house set in the rounded edge of a lawn that curved and spread haphazardly. Set in the lush grass, there was a stepping-stone path which meandered towards a child's swing.

'Chloe and Stacey will love that,' Nick said, 'and the boys when they're old enough,' and she nodded without speaking, battling against the mist of tears that had sprung to her eyes because she wouldn't be here with him to see it.

He looked sideways at her, and she blinked quickly, averting her face a little and pretending to take an interest in the old brick-built shed. 'That's big enough to store more than just garden equipment,' she said. 'It's huge.'

'That's true enough. I've some old nursery equipment back home in the loft—a trike and a pedal car, that sort of thing. I could put them in here.'

She looked at him quizzically. 'Have you been saving them all this time to pass on to your own children?'

'I guess. I never wanted to part with them, and when I was old enough to think about it I decided they might as well stay where they were.' He bent down to pull at a clump of weeds that were strangling a stray pansy. 'Has your Suzy thought about starting a family yet, or is she still intent on being a career woman? They had some problems over that, didn't they, with Ralph wanting children?'

Jessica moistened her lips carefully before answering him. 'They have their ups and downs, but they're still together, so I suppose they must have sorted things out. She's very keen on her work. She studied hard to be a graphic artist, and she loves what she does.'

'They've been married some time now, haven't they? How long has it been?'

'Ten years, I think.'

He stood up, brushing the dry earth from his hands. 'There's still time enough left for her to change her mind, I suppose?'

This time he looked at her directly, and she was proud that her voice held no sign of a tremor.

'I dare say.'

# CHAPTER ELEVEN

IT WASN'T too long after that visit that Jessica decided some things in her life would have to change. She had to accept that Nick could never be part of her life, and the kind of relationship they had at the moment was just too much of a drain on her emotions.

What she needed to do was to make a clean break. No more hankering after what might have been, no more using Matthew as an excuse. He'd been a good friend to her, he'd always listened and never once criticised, but it was time she stopped hiding behind him.

She would look for another job; that would be a start. She had been happy, here at the Soar Bridge centre, but it was time to move on, time to go back to doing what she had originally set out to do—working with children.

Acceptance had been slow in coming, but if it was to be that she couldn't have a family of her own then so be it; working with youngsters was the next best thing.

Already she had an application form for a job at the hospital, and when she had a few spare moments at work she pulled it out from her desk drawer and glanced through it. When Nick walked into the treatment-room, she pushed the paper to one side and looked up at him.

'You look like a dog with two tails,' she told him

with a grin. 'What's making you look so pleased?'

'Gemma's going into hospital for a transplant,' he announced. 'Her sister wants to donate one of her kidneys, and now is just about the best time it can happen for her. She's had a job offer, and she doesn't have to start it until after Christmas, so it's all systems go. It should be an ideal match, so all we have to do now is keep our fingers crossed that things go well for both of them.'

'Nick, that's wonderful news. I must go and see them. How soon shall we know?'

'It shouldn't be too long a wait. It all depends when Gemma's sister can make herself available and when the surgeon's list permits. Very soon, though.'

'I'm so pleased for Gemma.' She smiled contentedly, and Nick came and perched himself on the edge of the desk, picking up the application form she had been studying.

'What's this?' he asked, the beginnings of a small frown marring the smooth sweep of his brow. 'Are you thinking of leaving us?'

'I'm thinking about going back to children's nursing,' she said, watching his expression guardedly.

He nodded. 'That sounds like an excellent idea to me. I've always said it was what you were most suited for. In a way, you've been wasted here—you haven't really had to use your special skills.'

He clearly had no reservations about her leaving, and she tried to quell the pang of disappointment that gave her. He wouldn't miss her at all; it was only she who would feel any regret when she finally left.

'So what's to think about?' he asked, letting his glance skim through the job description. 'This sounds like just the thing for you.'

'I haven't quite made up my mind whether I want to work in a hospital again, or whether I'd rather do a health-visiting course. I'm quite taken with the idea of working with mothers and babies, based at a centre like this, but I'm not altogether sure what to do.'

'It would probably be less harrowing than working with very sick children,' he agreed, 'and the hours would certainly be more nine-to-five—no shifts or night work.' He glanced at the form again. 'You've some time before the application has to be in. I think you're right to give it some serious thought. Go home and sleep on it.'

'I shall.'

She meant to do that, over the next week or so, but her plans went slightly off course. One afternoon the familiar pains started up in her abdomen, and this time they were so severe that she went home early from work, something she'd never done before. She couldn't think of anything else but to try to do what she could to ease them. Usually a bath and mild painkillers helped, but not this time.

By morning she was feeling much worse, and she knew she wasn't going to be able to make it into work. She phoned in sick, feeling wretched and guilty for succumbing. It wasn't like her to give in to aches and pains, but it had never been quite like this before, and she knew she wouldn't have been able to cope with the clinics.

When late afternoon came, and she should have

been on her way to visit her parents, she gave her mother a call and told her she'd make it some other time.

Heather Reid let herself into the flat fifteen minutes later.

'Why on earth didn't you ring me before this, Jessica?' she chastised her. 'You look dreadfully pale. You know I would have come and done what I could for you. You and Becky are just the same: stubborn, independent, mulish. And what have you had to eat all day? Nothing, I'll bet.' She checked the plate on the bedside table. 'There, I knew it. A few biscuits.'

'I couldn't eat, Mum. You know what it's like sometimes—I feel sick. It won't be so bad when the pain eases off.'

Heather tut-tutted, fussing around the place like a mother hen. 'I'll make you some soup; that'll nourish you, and you might be able to keep that down.'

The doorbell went, and she hurried off to answer it, while Jessica lay back against the pillows and sighed, practising her deep breathing. It was probably the girl from the next-door flat, come to borrow something.

She wasn't at all prepared to see Nick's tall figure appear in the doorway. He had his briefcase with him, and she wondered if he was on call or whether he had stopped by on his way home. She couldn't remember what the rota was.

'How are you feeling?' he asked, coming to stand beside the bed and look down at her.

She struggled to sit up, and he gently pushed her back against the pillows. He sat on the edge of the divan and lightly ran the back of his hand over her forehead. It made her feel hot and bothered.

'I'm fine,' she said. 'I'll be up and about tomorrow. It's just a one-day stomach thing, that's all.'

He made a wry smile. 'A stomach thing? That might be what you've told them at the centre, but you aren't fooling me. It's practically a month to the day since you went through a similar stomach thing. And there was the month before that, and the month before that. Isn't it time you stopped trying to deny what's happening to you, and have someone sort it out? I want to help, Jessica. Why won't you let me help? Tell me what the doctor said, and we'll take it from there.'

'He's right, you know,' Heather said firmly, coming in with a tray and setting it down beside the bed. 'You should have told him a long time ago, and it makes no odds now, does it? There's no reason why he shouldn't know.' Her mother sent her a sharp look. 'The engagement's over; you're not together any more. You haven't been for almost two years. It's not as though it matters now.'

Jessica sucked in her breath sharply at the stark betrayal. What could she say, how could she keep him from delving too deep, now that her mother had split the nut wide open?

'Be-because of M-Matthew,' she stammered, 'is that what you mean?'

'You know what I mean,' her mother said.

Jessica thought about that. Perhaps she had a point, after all. Perhaps it didn't matter any more, now that she was preparing to leave the centre and take another chance at a separate life away from him. He wasn't concerned about her going. He had, in a way, exorcised her from himself that day, her birthday, and she ought to be able to tell him the truth now without any repercussions.

Her mother produced a paper serviette with a flourish. 'Get some of that down you,' she told her, flicking a glance towards the soup. 'I'm going to poke about the kitchen and see if you need stocking up on groceries.'

Jessica sighed as her mother left the room. 'She's annoyed because I didn't phone her earlier. I should have, I suppose. She loves making herself useful.'

'You were going to tell me what this is all about,' he said. 'It doesn't have to be personal. You don't have to think of it that way. I'm just a doctor, like any other. I've a professional interest.'

It hurt to hear him say that, but it was true now. He had wanted her while he couldn't have her, and since that day at his house he had made no attempt to get close to her. It was finished, done, and she felt bleak, empty inside, as though she had cried silently until all her tears had drained away.

'It isn't anything serious,' she told him. 'It's endometriosis. The tablets they usually prescribe don't suit me very well. It's just one of those things. I can live with it well enough. This last bout has been a little more painful, that's all, but I expect it will settle down.'

'Why didn't you tell me this before?'

'It wasn't important. It was my problem; I had to deal with it.'

He didn't say anything for a while, then, quietly, he said, 'I suppose you didn't tell me because you thought you couldn't have children, is that it? You didn't want me to know that.'

She gasped, the colour draining from her face. 'Why should you assume that?' she muttered. 'Some women with this condition are perfectly able to have children.'

'But in your case it isn't likely? Isn't that the truth of it?' He stated it as a fact, as though he knew all there was to know.

She clutched the duvet to her chest, gripping on to it as though it were a lifeline. 'I don't understand,' she whispered. 'I haven't told anyone, only my family, and they wouldn't——'

'I guessed,' he said. 'A few things puzzled me, and I began to put two and two together. It's the reason you quit hospital nursing. You'd been on neonatal and you had some kind of breakdown.' She sent him a swift, searching glance, and he said drily, 'I checked. They thought it was all the emotional upheaval of the broken engagement, coming so close to the wedding, but it was more than that, wasn't it?'

She twisted the cover of the duvet in her fingers, staring up at him with dark eyes. 'You didn't say anything about this to me. I had no idea you were thinking that way.'

'I wanted to be sure of my facts. The more I thought about it, the more everything started to fall into place. Your aunt and your sister have the same problem, don't they?'

'You couldn't know that,' she said, 'not for sure, not unless. . .unless. . .' She faltered, biting her lip.

'Becky told me about her own reasons for not having a family. Not the day we went over there, but after that. I rang her, and we chatted a while.'

'You *asked* her that? You rang her up specifically to ask her that?'

'No. I had a different reason for ringing her, and I wanted to say thanks for the evening. She volunteered the information, and after that it didn't take too much working out to see how the land lies elsewhere. There's a big age gap between you and Suzy, about nine years, if my calculations are correct, and your father once told me it wasn't because they preferred it that way.' His grey eyes probed hers. 'Are you afraid you're going to have the same problems? Have you had tests?'

'I've had tests,' she said in a voice so low that it could hardly be heard. 'I think my chances are the same as Suzy's and Becky's.'

He nodded. 'Then I think it's good that you've decided you can cope with the idea of working with children again. It shows you've accepted the way things are, that you're working on getting your life back together again. Will you go for health visiting?'

'Probably. If I can get on a course.'

'There shouldn't be any problem with that.'

He was so matter-of-fact about everything. She'd been worrying herself sick about his reaction, only it didn't bother him at all, because what he'd said was true—she was just like any other patient to him. What they'd had before was dead and gone. Finished.

'I suppose not.'

He stood up, and thrust his fingers into his trouser pockets, the edges of his jacket flicking backwards. 'Does Matthew know about the endometriosis and what it might mean?'

'Yes.'

'Has he known from the beginning?'

'Yes.'

He was silent for a while and she couldn't read what was in the darkness of his eyes. Then he said, 'You could have surgery. Wasn't that suggested to you?'

'It was. But there could be scar tissue, and that might lessen the chance of a pregnancy even more.'

'Not necessarily. Not if you had microsurgery.'

Her mouth made a cynical curve. 'The centres that do that are few and far between, aren't they? There are long waiting lists, and there's nothing available locally.'

'So we'll take you where it is available, or go privately.' He was thoughtful for a moment. 'I think privately might be the quickest.'

'It's out of the question,' she muttered, 'and besides, there would still be no guarantee that I might eventually conceive. It could all be for nothing.'

'There are never any guarantees. But it would stop the pain. And it isn't likely that the condition would come back, not if you went to see someone who is an expert in that kind of surgery. I think you should go ahead and have treatment.'

She shook her head. 'I can't afford private fees.'

'I can.'

'No,' she said. 'I won't take your money.'

'You're going to have to.'

She shook her head again. 'No. Nick, be realistic. I can't let you pay for my treatment, and anyway, you're in the throes of buying a house. That's enough of an expense on its own.'

'I can afford it,' he said bluntly. 'Besides, it may not come to that. I have contacts; I may be able to come up with someone who'll fit you into his list.' She opened her mouth to argue some more, and he held up a hand to shush her. 'Don't give me any more of that,' he rasped. 'I'm going to fix up an appointment for you with a micro-surgeon, one way or another, and I don't want to hear any more nonsense from you.' He stared at her, his mouth a firm line. 'For once, you'll do as you're told.' His glance flicked to the bedside table. 'And you can start by drinking the soup your mother made for you.'

He picked up his briefcase from the floor and opened it. 'I want you to take a couple of these painkillers, and then try to get some rest. I have to go now—I'm on call. I'll leave the bottle here, on your table, and you can take a couple more in four hours if need be.'

'Yes, Doctor. Of course, Doctor. Thank you very much, Doctor,' she recited politely. Then she spoiled it by giving a little sniff and choking back a gulp. 'It'll have to be a loan,' she muttered into the duvet. 'I *will* pay you back one way or another. It might take me a while, but I will do it.'

He glowered down at her. 'Soup,' he said

grittily. 'I'll send your mother in to deal with you.'

Jessica went into hospital a few weeks later. It was some distance from home, but her parents drove over to visit, bringing Suzy with them. Then Becky came, with Jack in tow, and there were a lot of hugs and kisses, and she felt a little overwhelmed by it all.

They'd rented a cottage a few miles away, so that they could come and see her each day. She wasn't quite sure why they'd all come, because it was hardly a major procedure she'd undergone, and she wasn't going to be in hospital for very long, but she was touched, all the same, by all the love and good wishes that surrounded her.

Nick came to visit, too, bringing flowers with him, and managing to squeeze a word in edgeways here and there, when her family would let him.

Matthew came on the second day. Nick and Suzy were in the middle of a friendly argument about the latest political scandal, but they stopped when he walked in. He bent towards her to drop a kiss on her forehead, and Nick stood up and walked out.

Nick came back a couple of days later, to drive her home, but he didn't say a word about Matthew, and she didn't want to broach the subject.

'I spoke to the surgeon while you were getting your things together,' he said, once they were settled into the car and pulling out on to the main road. 'He seemed very pleased with the way things went.'

'He's a very skilled man, isn't he? Nick, he said he would see Suzy if she wanted to contact him. He gave her his card. Did you have anything to do with that?'

'Why would I have anything to do with it?' He flicked a non-existent speck of fluff from his jacket sleeve. 'You must have mentioned her condition to him yourself. Didn't it come up in conversation?'

She looked at him doubtfully. 'I suppose that could be it. He did ask me if there was anyone else in the family who had similar problems.'

'There you are, then. That's your answer in a nutshell.' He turned the car on to the main road. 'You know, I think we should do something to celebrate your return home, maybe in a day or so, when you're feeling more yourself. It ought to be a triple celebration really, with me moving into my new home, and Gemma having her new kidney.'

She turned her face towards him eagerly. 'She's had it? You didn't say. . . When was this? How is she? How's her sister?'

He laughed. 'They're both doing fine, and the long-term prospects are excellent. It was done a couple of days before you came to the hospital. I didn't want to tell you then, in case you started to get agitated about it, because I know how close you are to her. I sent a card from both of us, and a basket of her favourite smellies—talcs and soaps and things.'

Her mouth curved softly. 'That was thoughtful of you, Nick; you are a lovely man. Remind me to kiss you some time.'

He didn't answer that, but kept his gaze on the road ahead, and after a while she said, 'How are you settling into your new house?'

'It went smoothly enough, given the rush I had to fit it in between surgery and being on call. I still haven't finished unpacking everything, and I keep finding there are things I need that are in the bottom of a crate somewhere. But it feels good to have a place of my own.' He smiled, throwing her a sideways glance. 'Actually, I need some advice on furnishings and fabrics and so on. I wondered if, when you're well enough, you'd come over and help me out.'

'I'd love to.' She'd grab any excuse going, just to be with him, because once she left the health centre and started her new course there was no saying she'd ever see him again. Over and over again she told herself it was for the best in the end, but it didn't make her feel any better. She felt thoroughly, hopelessly miserable at the prospect.

He came by the flat one evening a couple of days later, and drove her to the house.

'Go and make yourself comfortable in the living-room,' he said. 'At least it's fairly cosy in there. It's the one room that has more than a spartan amount of furniture in it, and I lit a fire earlier, so it should be nice and warm in there by now.'

'It's lovely, Nick,' she told him, sitting down on one of the deep, soft-cushioned settees and gazing around.

He had switched on a couple of table lamps, and light pooled gently over the polished table and low glass-fronted unit, lending a golden glow to the whole room. A fire burned in the hearth, orange and red flames flickering behind the gleaming brass grate.

'It'll take a while, but eventually I should manage to get the whole of the place fixed up so that it's more like a home than a house. I've managed to get hold of some swatches of material to give us some idea of curtains and so on, and there are wallpaper books and carpet samples in a corner somewhere.'

She turned to look for them, but he said, 'Not now. I didn't mean now—I thought we'd have that celebratory drink first, and a bite to eat. Just sit back while I bring the trays in.'

He came back from the kitchen with champagne on ice, and plates of hors d'oeuvres and small triangular-shaped sandwiches.

Her eyes shone as she took it all in. 'I can't believe I'm seeing all this,' she told him. 'Champagne? And these. . .' She gestured towards the plates. 'You didn't do all this yourself, did you?'

He laughed ruefully. 'I didn't, I'm afraid. I might be able to throw a few things in a frying-pan and cook up an omelette now and again, but my talents don't extend to anything as fancy as hors d'oeuvres. I just happen to be on very good terms with the manageress of our local bakery, so relax and tuck in.'

He poured champagne and came and sat beside her, passing her a glass of the sparkling liquid and clinking the glasses together in a toast. 'Health and happiness,' he said, and took a long swallow.

'Health and happiness,' she murmured, sipping her drink and wondering how she would ever be happy without him.

'I'll organise a proper housewarming when I've settled in and the decorating's finished,' he said, putting down his glass and leaning back. 'We'll have a look around later, and you can tell me what you think needs to be done.'

'I'm not well up on interior decorating,' she warned him. 'I know the kind of thing I like, but it might not suit you.'

'You have good taste,' he murmured. 'I trust your instincts. Jut choose as though it was your own home you were furnishing.'

She took another sip of champagne. 'It isn't, though, is it? I might make mistakes; it might not come out quite as we expected. I'm no expert——'

He shook his head lightly, a smile tugging at the corners of his mouth. 'Will you stop worrying? If it bothers you, look on it as a practice run, experiment a little.'

'Practice?' she echoed.

He shrugged. 'It isn't drastically important that it comes out right first time, is it? There are more important things in life than a few pieces of furniture and an assortment of fabrics. If they were the only problems I ever encountered I'd count myself a lucky man.' He took another swallow of his drink, glancing at her obliquely. 'Just imagine that I'm Matthew and you're choosing for your home together.'

He said it so casually, in such an unconcerned manner that he caught her off balance, and she paled rapidly.

'M-Matthew?' she repeated.

'Is that too difficult for you to do? You will be planning a home together one day, won't you?'

'A home?' She tried to clear her head but it seemed to be made of cotton wool. 'I—uh. . . well, I don't know quite. . .I mean, not in the near future. . .'

'Or not at all, in fact?'

Shocked, she stared at him with wide eyes. 'What did you say? I don't think——'

He looked at her directly, fixing her with his gaze. 'He was never really on the scene, was he? He was just an excuse, a convenient way for you to get out of marrying me.'

'How can you say that?'

'Jessica, I think it's time you came clean with me, don't you? When we were engaged, and I saw you wrapped up in his arms, I was convinced you were having an affair. You never denied it; you wanted me to go on believing it. But in fact, when I think back on that day, I recall that you were in his arms, and nothing much more was going on. You weren't kissing him, and he wasn't kissing you.'

He pushed his glass across the table with one long finger and reached for the champagne bottle, pouring himself another drink and topping up her glass. 'You were absolutely right a few weeks back when you said I jumped to conclusions. I did it all the time, I kept on jumping to conclusions, and you were happy for me to do that. I don't believe you ever told me a direct lie. You evaded, you went all around the houses, anything to keep the truth from me.'

'Why are you saying this to me?' she muttered, feeling the heat rising in her cheeks. 'Why now, Nick? You never said any of this before——'

'For more than a year I had that vision in my head, of you and him together. When I came to the Soar Bridge centre and found you there it felt as though I'd had a blow to the ribs from a huge fist. I didn't think clearly for a long while. But then I began to realise things didn't add up. Nothing added up. You were still seeing him, yet there was no ring on your finger; you weren't living together. It started signals going off in my head, because any man with half a brain would have snapped you up as fast as he could, and here was Matthew slow-pedalling. It didn't make any sense. Then Becky showed me the painting she'd done of you after we broke up, and there was something about your expression that caught my attention. It dawned on me that I'd been putting two and two together and coming up with all the wrong answers.'

Jessica thought back to that evening. 'You went with her to the studio. I remember. But that painting—if I looked different in any way it was because I'd been ill, Nick, and I'd given up my job, the work I'd trained for. . .'

'It's a very good painting, isn't it? A bleak and windswept scene—Becky's really captured it all on canvas, just as though she'd taken a photo.' He smiled. 'I asked her if she would sell it to me, and she refused point blank. She said I could have it with her love because it belonged with me. She's a very understanding woman, your aunt Becky.'

'You have it? Where?' She looked around the

room, but of course it wasn't in here, or she would have spotted it straight away.

'At the moment it's hanging on my bedroom wall, but we can put it wherever we decide it looks best.'

'We?'

'That's what I said. For the last few weeks that painting has been all I've had of you. Seeing it that first time gave me a glimpse of what you really felt when you broke off our engagement. I know there were other problems for you, but you were supposedly in love with Matthew, and he with you, and it would have to be a very strange relationship that left you looking so haunted.'

He reached for her hand and took it in his own, his thumb moving gently over her smooth skin in a light caress. 'I think, when you broke off our engagement, you still loved me. I think you still do. Can't you tell me the truth?'

A mist of tears stung her eyelids. 'I didn't mean to hurt you, Nick. I suppose I thought you would make a life for yourself without me.'

He shook his head. 'I can't do that. I tried, and it was sheer hell. And now that I've found you again I can't sit back and simply let you walk away. I love you, Jessica. I want you to be my wife. Will you marry me?'

'Oh, Nick, how can I do that?' She brushed away a tear before it could track down her cheek. 'I love you so much, but I can't marry you—it wouldn't be fair to you. You want a family so much, and there's no way I can promise you that. Even after the treatment I've had there's no way I can pin my hopes on giving you what you want.

I could try fertility treatment, but we would be waiting and hoping, and every time there was a disappointment I'd feel your loss. In the end you'd feel resentment towards me, you'd be bitter, and that could destroy us. It almost destroyed Ralph and Suzy. I don't want that to happen to you and me.'

'Why didn't you tell me this was how you felt? Why did you let me think you were involved with Matthew?'

'I thought you might say it didn't matter, that you'd love me anyway, and I know that would be true at first. Nick, I want a love that lasts a lifetime, I don't want to see it disintegrate because of lost hopes and recriminations. Can't you understand that?'

'Of course I understand.' He gripped her hands in his. 'But you have to try to understand things from my point of view. I know that we might not be able to have children, and I won't tell you that it wasn't important to me, because I should be lying if I did that. It was important, once, but if it means losing you, if it means living a life without you, then it will have to fade into insignificance. Because you are the most important thing in my life. You *are* my life, and this last couple of years without you has been sheer hell. I don't ever want to go through that again.'

He loosened his grip on her hands, but only to draw her closer, to gently stroke her face with his fingers and wipe away the slow trickle of tears. 'You can't compare us with Ralph and Suzy,' he said roughly. 'We're not starting out with any false hopes, either of us. If a child comes along we'll think of it as our little miracle, but we're not going to sit back and wait for it. Some awful things happen to people, we've both seen it; but you can't spend a lifetime crying about what's gone wrong. You have to get on with things, and that's what we shall do. We're both going to lead fulfilling lives, we can take joy in other people's offspring, through our work, through the family and friends. We'll have each other, and that's what matters more than anything else.'

He took her in his arms and held her close. 'Say that you'll marry me, Jessica. I promise I'll love you till the end of time.'

She gave him a watery smile. All the fight had gone out of her; all the anxiety she'd had in the past couple of years seemed to dissolve into fine mist in the face of his conviction. He was steadfast and true, and she ought to have known that he'd stand firm against adversity. He was that kind of man.

'I'll keep you to that promise,' she said quietly. 'I will marry you,' and as the smile curved his lips she traced it with her fingertips, and whispered, 'I love you more than I can say, more than I ever believed it was possible to love anyone.'

He kissed her then, a long, sweet and tender kiss, laying claim to her, body and soul, crushing her to him as though he would never let her go. When they came up for air much, much later he murmured huskily, regretfully, 'I have to let you go for just a minute. I have something for you.'

He released her for a second or two while he searched in his pocket, and then he produced a small velvet pouch. She gave a small cry as he opened it up and took out a familiar diamond engagement ring.

'You kept it,' she said, joy lighting up her face. 'Oh, Nick, I'm so glad.'

'When you gave this back to me,' he said, 'I thought my world had come to an end. But now I know that we've been through our testing time, and we've survived, we're both stronger for it.'

She held out her hand to him and he slipped the ring on to her finger.

'In just a few weeks' time,' he said, 'there'll be a band of gold right next to it. We'll be man and wife.'

'Man and wife,' she echoed softly as he drew her into his arms once more. 'I like the sound of that.'

Don't miss this year's exciting Mother's Day Gift Pack—4 new heartwarming romances featuring three babies and a wedding!

| | |
|---|---|
| *The Right Kind of Girl* | Betty Neels |
| *The Baby Caper* | Emma Goldrick |
| *Part-Time Father* | Sharon Kendrick |
| *The Male Animal* | Suzanne Carey |

**This special Gift Pack of four romances is priced at just £5.99**
**(normal retail price £7.96)**

 *Available:* February 1996 *Price:* £5.99 

MILLS & BOON

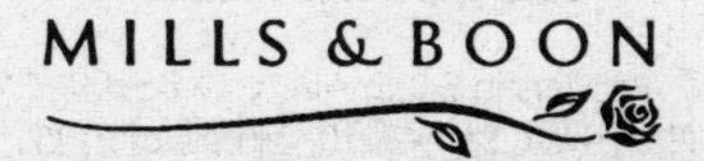

# Flower Power

**How would you like to win a year's supply of simply irresistible romances? Well, you can and they're free! Simply unscramble the words below and send the completed puzzle to us by 31st August 1996. The first 5 correct entries picked after the closing date will win a years supply of Temptation novels (four books every month—worth over £100).**

| | | |
|---|---|---|
| 1 | LTIUP | TULIP |
| 2 | FIDLADFO | |
| 3 | ERSO | |
| 4 | AHTNYHCI | |
| 5 | GIBANOE | |
| 6 | NEAPUTI | |
| 7 | YDSIA | |
| 8 | SIIR | |
| 9 | NNAIATCRO | |
| 10 | LDIAAH | |
| 11 | RRSEOIMP | |
| 12 | LEGXFOOV | |
| 13 | OYPPP | |
| 14 | LZEAAA | |
| 15 | COIRDH | |

**Please turn over for details of how to enter** ☞

Listed overleaf are 15 jumbled-up names of flowers. All you have to do is unscramble the names and write your answer in the space provided. We've done the first one for you!

When you have found all the words, don't forget to fill in your name and address in the space provided below and pop this page into an envelope (you don't need a stamp) and post it today. Hurry—competition ends 31st August 1996.

Mills & Boon Flower Puzzle
FREEPOST
Croydon
Surrey
CR9 3WZ

Are you a Reader Service Subscriber? Yes ❑ No ❑

Ms/Mrs/Miss/Mr ______________________

Address ______________________

______________________

______________ Postcode ______________

One application per household.

You may be mailed with other offers from other reputable companies as a result of this application. If you would prefer not to receive such offers, please tick box. ❑

COMP396
B